Acknowledgments

I first want to thank God for giving me the strength to continue writing even through the trials I have recently been through. I now understand that no matter what, my gift for writing can never be taken from me. To my parents, who supported and pushed my book, thank you. To my beautiful baby girl, Nyree Chrishelle, you're mommy's heart and soul. I love you so much! To my aunts and uncles who sold my books and bragged on me, thank you. I love you all. To my Aunt Madeline, who read the original version of *The Set Up* and loved it, I love you and am grateful for the close relationship I've developed with you. Paulette, thanks for being the good example I need. I do look up to you. Ms. Angie at Now and Then, thanks for loving and supporting my work. Also to Ms. Vernicia at V-Works, thanks for your support. To my cousin Angel, thank you for pushing my book in your salon. To Sharon Draper and Claudette Milner, thanks for your advice and support. To Debra Whitterson, thanks for the opportunity to do book signings with you two years in a row. To Barnes & Noble, Kenwood, Channel 19 morning news, 1480 WCIN, and 1230 The Buzz, thank you. Also, a big thanks to my editor Chloé A. Hilliard for working with me on this great project that I am proud to call my own. We did it again! To Cynthia Parker, thank you for breathing even more life into my story. I really enjoyed working with you. Thank you to Vickie and all the staff at Triple Crown. To all of my readers, thank you for begging for this sequel. I did it for you! I hope you all love it. And for every hater, old and new (you know who you are), get on your job, because there's much more where this came from!

-MM

the SET UP

Triple Crown Publications presents . . .

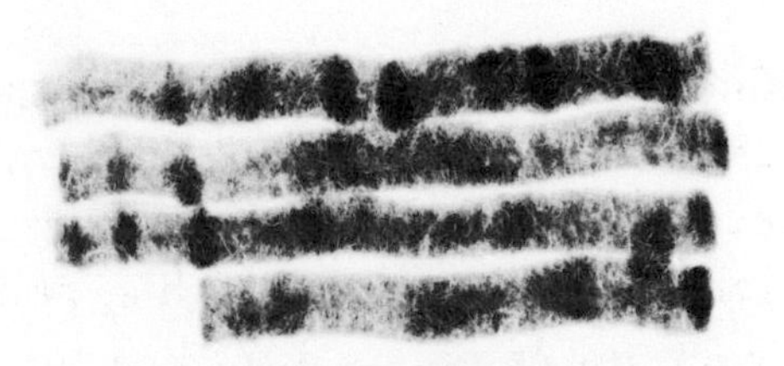

Prologue

"Come on, Moore. You're out of here." The guard unlocked my cell, which I sat in alone. Slowly, I got up. It had been three long years; I was no longer the sweet 18 year-old. I was 21 and had lost so much in my life, and finally I was being given back my freedom. I walked to the front gate where I was being released. I was expecting to see Damen and Zelle, but standing there waiting for me was Kayne. I froze up, unable to move. I couldn't believe it. I had waited for this day for so long. He walked over, kissed me and held me in his huge arms for a long time.

"I told you, one day…" He tilted my head up to look in my watery eyes. His face was the same but he looked older. His long cornrows were gone and he smelled so good. The last time I saw him he was still somewhat a boy but stand-

ing in front of me was a man, my man.

Finally I could shed tears of joy instead of tears of pain. I took advantage of the moment. The sky was bright and it was actually starting to snow. I inhaled the brisk air and felt alive. As I looked around, I spotted a Porsche.

"This us, baby," Kayne said with a grin, leading me to the car. Before he opened my door, he went to the trunk and pulled out a Gucci bag. Inside was a long, white Gucci leather. "It's cold out here, put this on."

"Where we goin'?" I asked, not really even caring. I was just grateful to be leaving prison. After three years, anywhere sounded like paradise.

"Home. It's me and you now for real."

"How you pull this off?"

"Zelle convinced Savellman to get me out last year."

"Last year?" I didn't understand why he was just now showing up. "So Savellman got me out, too?"

"Yeah, he came through after I paid him off. I know it took me a long time. Zelle wanted me to get my shit together first. He didn't even want me visiting you. I don't blame him, he just want you to have the best. Shit gon' be different now. We legal now. Zelle got a barber shop over on Vine. Business is good, he's been there about a year. I just opened up a club last month." Kayne went on to tell me about all of the things that had happened since I got locked up. No one was hustling anymore, either they were dead, locked up or gone straight. After hearing those stories I was kind of glad I was where I was instead of out fighting in the streets.

We pulled into the parking lot of a new apartment

building downtown. Kayne handed the valet the keys and took my hand, leading me to the entrance. We rode the elevator to the sixth floor, and Kayne opened the door to a spacious loft apartment.

"Surprise!" a group of people shouted as soon as I stepped in. I wanted to run and change, put some makeup on and fix my hair. But it was too late, everyone had already seen me in my baggy jeans, sweatshirt and jailbird cornrows. When I looked around at everyone who was there, it didn't matter how I looked. There was Damen, Zelle, Shayna, Kelly, who had a baby in her arms standing next to her boyfriend Shawn, Trina, Brell, Swag, my grandma, my aunt Angie, and right in the middle of the crowd, holding a huge cake that matched the banner over the window that said "Welcome Home Amina," was my mother. She still looked as beautiful as I had remembered her. Tears streamed down both our faces as our eyes met. She sat the cake down and we hugged for what seemed like forever. I thanked everyone and said a little speech then greeted them all, one by one, with a hug.

It was hard to believe that after all these years, and all I had been through, I was back home with everyone I loved. After I showered and changed into a Prada dress that Shayna bought me, we all got stuffed on the food my grandma had prepared.

"I made this just for you, Mi-Mi," she said, hugging me again.

I sat down next to Kelly and Shawn at the breakfast bar in my new kitchen. She showed off her five-carat diamond engagement ring and introduced me to her seven-month-old daughter named Rayonna. She was so pretty. I held her for a while and then I went to talk to everybody else from the hood.

Swag was about to get signed by a big record company in New York. Brell had his own place in Avondale, and was working in Kayne's club located in Newport. Trina was in her third year at Florida State. She had flown in just for my homecoming.

When I talked to my mom, she told me everything that had happened with Markus. They had lived in Texas for a year. Finally, she left him and came home to live with my grandma until she bought a house in College Hill.

After getting over the initial shock of seeing everyone, I was surprised by how beautiful my new home was. "I love it," I told Shayna who revealed that she had designed the whole thing for Kayne. She went on to tell me about how she and Damen got married. I wondered why no one had written to tell me about it. But it didn't matter now. I was home and that was all that mattered.

For some reason, Zelle couldn't take his eyes off of me the whole night. We really didn't get a chance to talk much but I knew that he was just happy to see me smile again.

"It's time for presents!" Shayna shouted, getting everyone's attention.

All the presents were mostly clothes and some cards with money. I was grateful for each gift. My mom gave me a locket with my name engraved on it, and a touching card that caused me to cry again. Damen handed me the keys to a 2006 Mercedes Benz. I was back in style. Zelle gave me a diamond charm bracelet with my initials, a heart and a

crown.

Then finally it was Kayne's turn. He handed me a small ring box. I opened it and was almost blinded by the eight-carat pink diamond ring.

"This ain't just a promise ring, I'm ready to make it official." He slid the ring on my finger and kissed me on the lips softly. I was speechless and so was everyone else around me. Silently, they waited for my response.

"Yes," I was finally able to whisper. Everyone went wild.

After everyone left, Kayne took me to his club. It was huge, with three bars and two levels. No one was there but us so he turned down the lights, turned on a slow song, and opened a brand new bottle of Cristal. We sat in a VIP section. He pulled me close and whispered in my ear.

"Amina, you've made me the happiest man in the world."

"If you the happiest man, then I must be the luckiest woman," I said, turning to kiss him. My mind flashed back through everything that had happened in the past four years. *This is how it's supposed to be. Me and Kayne together with money to last and if I had to do it all over, I would still be down*, I thought.

* * * *

I opened my eyes to find that I was still lying in my cell. It had all been a dream. Three years hadn't really passed, it was still May 10th, 2004. I looked on the floor and saw a letter sitting there. The guard must have dropped it off while I was asleep.

Dear Amina,

I don't know how to tell you this, but I'll do my best. I called Terrance today and didn't get an answer. When I called his sister, she told me that he had been arrested for reducing her husband's years in jail. He's facing 45 years. Fortunately, no one's found out about him helping Zelle out. Unfortunately, Zelle was the only one that made it out with his help. If I could, I would pay any amount to keep you from the next 21 years in jail. But I can't. Zelle is opening a barber shop downtown, so he'll be visiting often, and I promise to visit every chance I get. I love you so much. Your brother and I promise we will never abandon you. Never. Stay strong.

Love,
Daddy

I ripped the letter into tiny pieces and let out a piercing scream, fell to the floor and started pounding my fists into the cold, hard concrete. Four guards rushed to my cell. I continued screaming as they tried to force me under their control. I threw a complete fit. They dragged me to solitary confinement where I spent a whole night in tears.

When I finally drifted off to sleep, I had another dream about Kayne. This dream picked up where the last left off, and featured our wedding day. Of course it caused me to wake up screaming like a mad woman again. I punched and kicked the walls. I pulled my hair and scratched my face.

I was on suicide watch for two weeks. I was constantly hearing voices, so many of them. They were fucking with my head. The first voice I heard was my mother's. *Stop trying to mess up a good thing for me, I love him.* It echoed so loud I was sure the guards could hear her, too. I tried to block her out. She repeated the same words over and over. I screamed and pulled at my hair.

Just when I began to get rid of her voice, other ones came to haunt me. *Bitch, shut the fuck up!* Tino shouted in my ear. I kicked and screamed, trying to escape the memory of him raping me. *I'm sorry, I have to go back to Chicago, it's what's best for me,* Damen whispered. "Daddy, don't leave me again..." I cried, curling up into a ball rocking myself back and forth. The voices only got worse. *I'm gonna get his ass, just like I got Zelle.*

"Bitch! I'ma get you!" I screamed at someone who wasn't there.

Then I heard Shadow. *Look, let's just do it a little easier. Let's just forget the poison and do stabbing instead.* My crying ceased as I realized what I had done – I'd had somebody murdered. I began apologizing to no one in particular over a hundred times.

"I'm sorry...I'm so sorry..." I cried until Kayne's voice came to soothe me.

Yeah, I love you, if I didn't I wouldn't be doing all this. It'll be three months on the 16th, and it's something different than it is with other females. I listened for more from him, as I lay on the dirty mattress letting the wet tears dry on my face. *What you know about hustlin' anyway? You crazy if you think I'ma have you out there like that. It ain't*

worth you riskin' yo' life. I'll be aight. I nodded in agreement as Kayne told me these words, this time. *Go get you a place like I said. I gotta go, I love you. And stop cryin', this ain't the last you gon hear from me.* I wiped my tears. I believed him.

"Ok, I'll wait on you, baby, I ain't goin' nowhere. I promise when you get home, I'll be here." I failed to realize that it was too late.

The nurse came in and handed me a small plastic cup with two pills inside, and a cup of cold water.

"I'm feeling better, I don't need this," I told her, handing it back to her.

"Yes, you do, Amina. You've been doing good on taking your medication the last three days. Please don't give me trouble now."

I stared at the pills. "I talked to Kayne, he wants me to get myself a place to stay. He wants me to just wait on him. It's gonna be hard, but I can do it. Three years really ain't that long, is it?" I looked at her for reassurance, she looked annoyed.

"Not really. Three years flies by. Take your pills, Amina."

"Do they have any of those apartment magazines here? I need to find somewhere cheap right now, so I can pay for Kayne's lawyer."

"If you take the pills, I'll get you one."

"I don't want this damn medicine! What the hell I need medicine for? Get me one now!"

"Amina, I won't do it until you take your medication," she said calmly, standing directly in front of me with both hands on her hips.

"I ain't takin' shit. I'm tired of being treated like some

fuckin' nutcase, I'm leaving!" I threw the pills and the water on the other side of the room and pushed her out of my way. She fell backwards onto the medication tray that she pushed in with her. I ran for the huge steel door, kicked it and an alarm sounded. I ran to the other side of the room. I already knew there was no other exit, but I searched for one anyway. I only found the same cement wall I'd been staring at for the last two weeks.

Three guards and another nurse rushed in and straddled me to the floor. I couldn't kick or punch because the guards had me held down. The nurse bent down and shot me in the right arm with a needle filled with a clear liquid. I blacked out right away.

* * * *

When I woke up, I found myself in a room with padded walls wearing a straight jacket. I had been placed in a mental institution. The voices kept coming; I was also having more dreams. It was like I was living my life through these dreams. They were all in order. Eventually they ceased, and the voices stopped, too. I was so relieved. When they did, I was transferred to a bedroom with a Spanish girl who loved to cut her wrists. She never said anything but I didn't care because neither did I.

Every day at ten a.m., I attended a two-hour meeting with other girls my age. After that was lunch. I ate a turkey sandwich, plain Lay's chips, an apple and a choice of milk or water every single day. After lunch I met with my private psychiatrist who reminded me so much of my mother.

Believe it or not, I liked her. She encouraged me to use the dreams in a positive way. I agreed to try.

I begged her to get me in touch with Kayne so I could write him.

"I can't do that, Amina. Writing him will do you no good. A simple letter is what got you here in the first place," she told me.

After that I began to hate her, just like I hated everyone else there. I shut everyone out, I didn't talk at the meetings and I refused to speak to my psychiatrist.

My punishment was no visitors until Christmas. That was seven whole months, but what did I care? Damen and Zelle didn't even know where I was. To my surprise though, they both showed up Christmas day but at different times.

Zelle gave me the exact same charm bracelet as he did in my dream. I started crying hysterically. He was then forced to leave, and I was sent to my room where I continued crying until Damen showed up that evening with the best Christmas present I could ask for — my mom.

"Baby, I'm so sorry," was the first thing she said, taking me into her arms.

Damen hugged me, too, then we all sat down in the visitor room.

I told my mom everything, starting from the night I left home. When I finished, she was in tears right along with me.

"I'm so sorry. I never should have let you leave. I was so stupid," she said, holding me again. An hour had passed and my visiting time was up. I went back to my room feeling better but still not willing to talk to anyone.

* * * *

Almost three years have passed since Kayne and I were separated, and sometimes I still have dreams and wake up in a fit. But after a while, they just got tired of punishing me because it never helped.

Damen visits every major holiday, just like he promised. Shayna always comes along. My mom bought a house as close to the center as she could, and spends as much time with me as she can. My grandma visits, too.

Zelle had a little boy named Canoray. He brings him by every chance he gets but I've never seen the mother. I think they're separated.

A week ago, I overheard two nurses talking about someone not being able to visit me, because it would cause me to go into withdrawal again. They never said a name, only "he." When I saw Zelle yesterday, he told me they were talking about Kayne. Instead of crying or throwing a tantrum, I looked him in the eye calmly. "Just tell him that I love him, and if we ever got the chance to be together again, I would still be down." I meant every word of it.

Chapter 1

Friday—June 2, 2006

I couldn't believe it. I was back in front of the judge who tried my case the first time. I had been through a lot since I'd been on lock down, but I was never going to let up that the charges filed against me were false. They charged me with selling narcotics to an undercover officer, which was true, but they were also labeling me as the leader of a major drug ring, like I was the female Suge Knight of the streets. Truth be told, I was scared shitless when they hit me with the maximum sentence of twenty-one years. That was some bullshit because it was my first offense. My attorney was shady and went to prison over some crazy shit he did, so I was left with nobody. Only when I went into the mental institution did someone finally listen to me. I knew I wasn't crazy, but under the circumstances, I lost it, and right-

fully so. I learned that crazy people got treated better than people in prison, and if that was what it took, I'd babble like a muthafucka making no sense whatsoever.

After a visit from my father, I learned that the undercover cops who arrested me were actually crooked cops. They were known for handling high-end drug busts then keeping the product and money for themselves and distributing it. Ain't that some shit? After multiple arrests, the defense attorneys began to see similarities between each case. Every person arrested had the same claims about the officers, that the allegations were false, and the reports didn't add up. The officers reported finding hundreds of thousands of dollars and tons of drugs on each set up, but when evidence was tagged and it was time to go to court, the shit was gone. The District Attorney was forced to look at every drug case, which resulted in a conviction of the two officers. Mine was one of them—thank God.

"The State versus Moore," the judge spoke sternly. "Please stand for the court."

I stood, with my heart beating strongly. All eyes were on me.

"After reviewing your case and considering the lack of evidence and the charges that are now pending against the officers who arrested you, the courts have decided to overturn your sentence. We have no reason to hold you here." Cheers from my family rang out, and I broke down in tears. "Because you were affiliated with known drug dealers, you will be placed on probation for the next five years." Then the judge spoke in a softer tone. "Miss Moore, the justice system is not perfect, and we do make mistakes."

"Amen!" I heard someone say.

"An apology will not take away the years that you have served, nor replace the tears that you've shed. You've been given another chance at life. This time, please make the right decision."

"Thank you, Your Honor, I will."

"Also," the judge spoke, "under the new false imprisonment law, you will be compensated for your time here."

I was glad to hear that because I needed some cash.

"Miss Moore, you are a free woman."

I sobbed uncontrollably when I heard those words.

Once I got back to my room at the crazy house, I lay down on my bed, too shocked to get my shit together. My sentence was overturned. I couldn't believe it.

Getting back to the real world couldn't come quickly enough.

Chapter 2

Tueday—July 4, 2006

After spending two years in a mental institution, I was finally home. I was labeled "mentally stable" on May 22, 2006, granted parole by the court system on June 2, and by the Fourth of July, I stood at the window of my brand new condo at the EdgeCliff, sipping a martini and gazing at the fireworks dancing in the night sky over the Ohio River. They seemed to be welcoming me home. I had to beg Zelle to talk our pops, Damen, into purchasing the condo for me. He agreed only because it was better than sending me money for rent every month and not owning the spot—a waste of money as we both saw it.

My best friend through thick and thin, Kelly, came to the rescue and took on the job of turning my condo out. I'm talking about only the finest of furniture, electronics and

appliances. The interior design was so hot I didn't even know if I could have done a better job myself. She even went as far as to purchase a beautiful white bear skin rug that complemented my pale blue suede sectional sofa like no other. The white glass engraved mirror that hung on the main wall of my living room was perfect, and even four inches bigger than my 42-inch Sony plasma television complete with dual surround sound for our entertainment. The rest of the living room space was taken up by two round, all-glass end tables and four pale blue and white marble designed vases. I loved that she decorated that room using my favorite color schemes.

My bedroom wasn't short-changed either. Inside was a king-sized, cherry-wood-framed bed with a butter-colored leather headboard and a matching cherry wood dresser with mirror. My bed was adorned with a gorgeous cream satin comforter with 800-count silk sheets, and matching satin pillows of various sizes. On the wall was a 32-inch Sony plasma television.

My bathroom was filled with delicious-smelling vanilla candles. When I had first come home, all the candles were lit and led me to my Jacuzzi tub, which was spilling over with white rose petals. My bathroom was like heaven, and I spent the majority of my time relaxing there and getting more of a perspective on my life.

As a thank you, I fixed dinner and drinks as Kelly and I watched the fireworks from my balcony. Only a true friend would lay out my place to look even better than her own. I knew it would probably be a while before she got to redecorate her own home, which she shared with my brother,

considering the amount of money she had hit him up for to decorate my spot. Kelly and Zelle had been together ever since she left Shawn in '04 because he was fucking around.

It tripped me out when I first saw them together. I remembered Kelly crushing on him back when we were seventeen. I was happy for them, though. Zelle took care of Kelly and moved her into his three-bedroom high-rise apartment downtown with his two-year-old son, Canoray. Zelle got custody of Canoray after his mama, Tracy, got turned out on crack and left the boy home alone for two days. Now she was only allowed supervised visits.

As far as things between me and my brother, we had a lot of catching up to do, but we were still tight as ever. I was so proud of him for getting out of the game. I didn't ever want to be separated from him again. He was still the same overprotective Zelle, and I wanted to make him proud of me. His barber shop was going strong for the second year. He had moved up from four chairs to seven and was even looking into opening another location somewhere in the 'burbs.

Damen, on the other hand, was so strict I felt like I was still locked up. He told me he didn't want me getting back in the habits of my old lifestyle, because he was afraid I would make the same mistakes. I knew he was just being a good father, and I was grateful for that now that I was older. If he had spent the last two years where I had, he would know that nothing in the world would make me go back to hustling in the streets. My mother agreed with Damen and tried to talk me into moving in with her until I got on my feet. I explained to her that I just wanted to be alone after being deprived of all of my privacy and freedom for two years.

* * * *

Having to report to a P.O. every week was a pain. I hated the one who was assigned to me. Her name was Mary Kettleson. She was old, dry and so damn annoying. Her vocal cords were warped from smoking cigarettes. The sound of her slow, whining, raspy voice annoyed me so much I had to get mentally prepared before stepping into her small, stuffy and cluttered office. I was running ten minutes late to my second appointment since my release. When I finally made it to her office, she said just what I expected.

"Amina, I'm going to need you to work on being here on time."

"Sorry." I rolled my eyes. It was only my first time being late.

"Okay." She continued looking over my paperwork over the rim of her red framed glasses which rested on the tip of her nose. I stared at her, waiting for the questions to begin. Not only was she obnoxious, but she was really a chore to look at. Her brown hair was never combed, her skin was wrinkled and pale and apparently no one had ever taken the time to advise her on how to apply makeup. Her mascara was always clumped together and her eyelashes looked like two tarantulas sitting on her face.

"Have you been looking for a job?" she asked, looking over the rim of her glasses again.

"Yes, I'm actually on my way to work after I leave here. My brother helped me get a job at a clothing store in Clifton. It's my first day."

"Great, I'll need the name, address and phone number of the store, and I'll give you this form to have signed by a supervisor and returned to me at your next appointment."

"The store is called The Shop," I told her even though she didn't ask. I was just so excited about having my first real job.

"The Shop ..." she repeated to herself as she wrote it down. "Okay, once you get all of the pertinent information, just bring it back to me with your paperwork."

"I will."

"Alright, how much money will you be making weekly? Hourly?"

"Nine-fifty an hour. That's about three hundred a week." I rolled my eyes at the thought.

"You know, that's actually better pay than what most people on parole can find. You should really thank your brother."

"Yeah, I have."

"How are your brother, mother and father adjusting to you being home?" The bitch was getting all in my personal business. If I was working and minding my own business, why couldn't she do the same?

"Everything is great with all three of them. They're happy to have the old Mina back." I smiled.

"Great!" she said, smiling. "You seem to be doing well so far. I won't need a urine sample from you until next week. Hopefully that will continue to come back clean." She

threw me a look before continuing. "How about your friends and associates? Have you been keeping good company?"

"I've only been with family since I've been home. They're all I have."

"That's definitely true. How about the infamous Keon NaCore? Have you spoken to him?"

"No, and I don't plan to," I told her without one blink.

"Alright." She jotted something on a piece of paper. "Amina, we're done here. I just need you to return that form next Wednesday and be prepared for a drug screen."

"Okay, thanks."

I walked out to my car with her last question lingering in my mind. Had I seen Kayne? No, but would I see him? And if I did, would I know what to say or do? Could I even handle the sight of him? Yes, I still loved him, but most of me hated him, and at the time I didn't really know why I still cared. I was proud of the progress I'd made with my life, and whether Kayne came back around or not, I was going to keep moving in the right direction. I had made myself the most important person in my life, and this time around, no man would change that. I knew Kayne had loved me, but I had to ask myself ... would he have given up his whole life and well-being for my sake?

Chapter 3

Monday—July 10, 2006

I parked my pearl white Denali directly in front of The Shop and got out, dreading having to work for such bullshit pay. No hourly job could add up to the expensive lifestyle I was used to, but it was a step in the right direction. I was determined to get my shit together, because easy money ain't always good money. I promised myself that I would never put myself in such a vulnerable position that I would have to make bad choices, even if it was out of love. Most of all, I would never make a drop for anyone else again, no matter what. In my eyes, being legal was the new hot thang to be.

My bank account was sitting real heavy thanks to Zelle and Damen anyway. My mother even contributed a few thousand. I knew I had nothing to worry about, and it felt

good to be straight. Everyone wasn't lucky enough to be taken care of fresh out of prison, but I was. So before I got out of my car, I took a deep breath and put a smile on my face. Things were looking up.

It was only eleven o'clock in the morning and it was already ninety-two degrees outside. As soon as my feet hit the ground in my black stilettos, I wished I had worn more comfortable shoes.

"Hey, Amina. You early ain't you?" Mike commented as I walked into the air conditioned store front with a sigh.

"Yeah, I had a ten o'clock appointment. It didn't last long, so I just came straight here."

"That's cool. You can go ahead and rearrange the window display for me before I open up."

I followed Mike to the back where he gave me the clothes he wanted displayed. He had already trained me the week before at my second interview so I knew the first day would be fairly easy. He didn't seem too demanding or cocky like a lot of street niggas with money could be. I liked him, but not in a sexual way. He was fine, but I had already decided to keep business separate from pleasure, mostly out of respect for Zelle.

There was a slight lunchtime rush on Short Vine. I watched from the window as I dressed the mannequins. I liked putting together the window display. Mike had some of the hottest clothes in Cincinnati. I added my own personal touch to the display, making it almost impossible to ignore the window. As I worked, my mind wandered back to Kayne.

"Keon, I'm over here!" I heard someone shout.

An alarm went off in my head when I heard his name. I dropped the clothes in my hand and looked up desperately, ready to run to him before it registered in my head that the voice was a female one.

"Come on, let's go. I'm hungry," she said to him from a black Lexus SUV parked directly next to my truck.

"Why ain't you tell me you was going to the car?" he asked as he got in the passenger's side. She mouthed something I couldn't hear and kissed him on the lips the way I had dreamed of kissing him again. As they pulled away, I was completely frozen. The only thing moving was the single tear falling slowly down my face, tickling my cheek. I was too numb to wipe it away.

"If you're done you can get money for the register. I'm about to unlock the doors in a minute," Mike said, pulling me out of my trance.

"Okay, let me go to the restroom. I'm sorry." I covered my mouth with my hand. "I feel really sick all of a sudden." I ran to the restroom in Mike's office. The small bathroom seemed to be spinning in circles. I had to regain control before I lost it. I couldn't leave—it was my first day.

I took six deep breaths, a weak technique I had learned in treatment, but nothing could get rid of the bruise on my heart. Images of her kissing him played over and over in my head. The sound of her calling my man's name taunted me as I tried to clear my head. I remembered her face, assuring myself that I would find and kill her. She was lighter than me, with her hair cut close to her head in a Halle Berry style. She had a Marilyn Monroe piercing over her lip, and bright hazel eyes.

Since when does Kayne like girls with short hair? I thought to myself, recalling how he would always run his hands through my hair when I laid my head on his lap while he watched SportsCenter.

"Maybe he wants somebody who won't remind him of me. He has to be missing me," I said to myself out loud, believing my own words. I felt myself going insane again.

Mike knocked on the door, snapping me back to reality. "You okay in there?"

"Yeah, I'm fine," I lied. "I think it might have been the McDonald's I ate this morning."

"You need to go home?"

"No, I can't go home. It's my first day," I reminded him after coming out with the most pitiful look I could muster.

"Go ahead. I'll be cool, but I'll need you first thing tomorrow. So go get better for me, shorty."

"Thanks, Mike. I'm so sorry."

"It's cool. Just be here tomorrow."

"Okay." I walked to the car, relieved that I had been given the chance to spend this awful moment at home alone.

* * * *

It was freezing inside my apartment. I kicked off my shoes and collapsed on my sofa. I didn't even bother to turn the AC down—there was no way I could get myself off the couch. The phone rang, and I let the machine pick up.

"Mina, I talked to Mike," said Zelle. "He told me you went home sick. If you get this message, call me. I'll be over

to check on you after I close tonight."

After waking up an hour later, I decided to call him back.

"Hello?" Zelle answered.

"Hey, Zelle, I got your message. I been throwing up ever since I got home. I think I might have food poisoning."

"What you eat?" He sounded concerned.

"I had some McDonald's earlier this morning. You know, all that grease might have done it."

"I told you about eating that stuff, girl. You want me to bring you some soup or something when I leave?"

"That's alright. I got some here I can heat up real quick."

"Okay, get some rest and call me when you get up."

"I will." I hung up only to get another call. This time, it was Kelly.

"What's up? Zelle told me you was sick. You need me to come over?"

"I ain't sick, but you can come over. We need to talk."

"Right now?"

"Yeah. Right now."

"I'm on my way." Kelly was still my best friend, so I had to tell her what was up. And believe it or not, the bitch had actually learned how to keep a secret, so I trusted that she wouldn't tell Zelle.

The look on Kelly's face when I told her about seeing Keon "Kayne" NaCore and his girl scared me. She didn't even respond. It was like she already knew. I hadn't spoken Kayne's name to anyone since the day Zelle had told me he had come to visit me in the institution. Kelly looked worried that I was about to lose it again, but I was acting perfectly sane in my eyes.

"Did you hear me, Kelly?" I asked. "I saw Kayne, and he looked even better than I remember him." I tried to snap her out of her silence, but I still got no response. "Girl, believe me, I ain't worried 'bout that chick he with if that's what you thinking. I'll be fine, and I'll get him back. Believe that," I said to a mute Kelly as I sat down on the couch. I was fidgeting with my nails, waiting for her to spit out whatever she was holding in. The TV played low, and Kelly sighed, then finally spoke.

"Amina?" She spoke so low, it was barely above a whisper. I only stared at her. I already knew I wasn't about to hear good news.

"Sweetie, I think you've done a good job of getting over Kayne, but you need to keep moving. There's way too much pain there, Mina, please don't bring that back on yourself. He ain't changed. He still out here hustlin' instead of layin' low or going legal like Zelle. Don't get caught back up, you been through too much."

"Kelly, how do you know he ain't working on getting legal? That shit don't happen overnight. And I know you don't think I'm 'bout to sit back and let some other bitch have the man I literally gave my life for. I know you know better. If Kayne hustling is the only good reason you can come up with for me not to get back with him, you better try a little harder." I changed the station to "*BET*" and turned up the volume. I noticed Kelly's silence. Yeah, no come back. Didn't think so.

Then she dropped a bomb with absolutely no warning.

"His girl is seven months pregnant, and they're engaged." She looked away, unable to face the look of devastation on my face.

"Kelly, tell me you lying!" She said nothing. "Kelly, tell me you lying!"

"I'm sorry, Mina, I can't tell you that."

"Is that why Zelle and him don't speak anymore?"

"Yeah. I'm so sorry. Mina, I didn't want to tell you. You was doin' so good." She looked about ready to cry. My mouth opened, but no more words came out. I wanted to know details, but I couldn't bear them at the moment. I completely let my guard down and broke down in Kelly's arms.

"How could he do this to me?" I cried as Kelly rubbed my back. "How could he move on so fast? How could he forget about me?"

Kelly held me and allowed me to get all of my emotions out as I bawled harder than I ever had in my entire life.

Chapter 4

Tuesday—July 11, 2006

All I felt like doing was staying in bed all day feeling sorry for myself, but I knew Mike needed me. I dragged myself out of bed at nine o'clock to take a long bath and make it to work by eleven.

I'm not sure what the occasion was, but it seemed to be raining ballers all day long in the store. I was actually enjoying the attention I received from every male customer who came through, but I still turned down all of their attempts to get my number or leave me theirs. Kayne weighed heavily on my mind.

After work, I met Zelle at Red Lobster. He said we needed to talk, and we hadn't spent much time together since I'd been home, so I was looking forward to dinner with him.

After ordering our food and a few minutes of small talk,

Zelle all of a sudden became quiet.

"What's wrong?" I asked.

"Can I ask you something?"

"Of course."

"What exactly did Kayne tell you about his case two years ago?"

"What do you mean?" I was confused.

"Why was he facing only four years? Did they find guns, drugs? What happened?"

"The lawyer told me they hadn't found anything, but he was looking at three to four years. I figured the police had just been watching him for a long time, or maybe he had been set up by an informant." I wished he would get to the point.

"Mina, I know you not all off into the law, but everybody knows without evidence there's no case."

"So what are you getting at?" I threw my fork down, frustrated.

"What I'm saying is Kayne couldn't have been telling you the whole story." He paused and looked me dead in the eyes. I waited for him to continue. "They didn't lock him up for having too much money, they ran in his spot. You know how they wanted information from you about him and Wess, and where they kept their shit?"

I nodded my head, recalling the day my grandma told me they wanted information about their "crack houses." I had no idea what they were talking about, but now it was all making sense.

"Well, Kayne made a spot out of these two chicks' house out in Colerain. They're cousins named Shalauna and

Marla. I used they crib for about a month before I figured out that shit was hot, too many different niggas comin' through. When I stopped comin' through I tried to get Kayne to back off, too. He told me shit was cool and that I was just noided. He thought it was safe because it was out the way, but I still didn't trust it. Suburban police can be worse than city cops. Anyway, to make a long story short, when y'all was in Puerto Rico, DART busted the door down and found everything. Shalauna had already established that if something happened, she wanted money for bail and a lawyer, but she would take the case. But as soon as they read her the numbers, that bitch sang like a bird. Kayne believed she was street, but obviously not street enough."

"So they let her go?"

"No, she did a year and a half, but for having that shit in her name she should have done much longer. I don't know exactly how much dope they found though."

"What about Marla?"

"Marla did a little bit of dirt, but she worked and was in nursing school at Cincinnati State. She was hardly there. She moved out before all this went down. I guess she smelled what was coming, too."

"Was he fuckin' around with either one of them at the time?" I asked, already knowing the answer.

"Like I said, I stopped going over there, but when I was there you and Kayne didn't even know each other yet."

"I saw him with a girl yesterday at the store. I already know it's Marla, so you don't have to cover for him."

"You saw Kayne yesterday? Did he see you?"

"No."

"What happened?" He sounded shocked and concerned. I decided to play cool.

"Nothing. I didn't speak to him. It's obvious he's moved on. I won't intrude."

"Amina, it's me you talking to. What's up? How did you *really* feel about seeing him with her?"

Tears filled my eyes as my mind replayed the memory. "I felt stupid," I answered honestly. "Like I made the biggest mistake of my life by loving him. And now I find out he was with this bitch all along."

"I never said that, Amina," Zelle attempted to correct me.

"This is some bullshit!" My hurt turned into anger and stopped the tears from dropping.

"I'm sorry, baby girl. I hate that you had to see him with another woman. I haven't talked to that nigga, so I don't really know shit about him and her, but what I do know is he cared about you when y'all were together, and you know I would never lie to you. But if you do see him again, be cool. You been doing good ... don't let nothing fuck that up."

"Hopefully, I won't."

"What do you mean, hopefully?" Zelle raised his eyebrow and looked at me inquisitively in an attempt to read my mind. "Don't let nothing fuck that up," he repeated, this time more sternly.

"I won't, Zelle."

He seemed satisfied with my answer.

"Shit will work out the way it's supposed to."

"You're right," I confirmed.

"You home now, you got your family, you doin' good, and I'm proud of you."

"Thanks, Zelle, I needed to hear that."

"I been wanting to tell you that for a while, but I just been so busy. I'm glad I'm finally able to sit down and spend some time with my baby sister. I missed you like crazy while you was away." He smiled.

"I missed you, too." My eyes filled up with tears again as I looked at Zelle. "I really feel like I let you down. You taught me so much, but I failed to use anything you taught me to my advantage."

"It's not your fault," Zelle said compassionately.

"I can't get that day out of my mind." I closed my eyes and put my hands up to my head. "The cops, the duffle bags, those handcuffs." I shook my head, trying to erase the memory, then opened my eyes. "I just still can't believe I didn't know I was being set up. It's so funny how I spent so much time around drug dealers and really knew nothing about the game. I even let Derrick convince me that what I was doing was no big deal. I told him I needed fifteen grand, and he made it sound easy to get it in three weeks. Three weeks, that should have been the key. Three weeks, a true hustler can make that in a few days. Three weeks is enough to have someone under surveillance.

"I should have known something because he was too eager to show me how to do shit first hand. Worst of all, my dumb ass didn't even know how much money the shit was worth! A kilo back then was going for a good twenty-two thousand, and I went to pick up five thousand petty dollars? Zelle, where the fuck was my head?"

"Mina, if you ask most females how much a brick is worth most of them would have no clue. Consider it a worthwhile mistake because if the trade was any more than that, we wouldn't be sitting here talking now."

I thought about Zelle's reasoning. "You're right. Nigga tried to be slick along with them dirty-ass cops. More of them dirty bastards need to be investigated. They got the perfect legal hustle on an illegal trade. Arresting folks, taking their shit and writing up a bogus report. That shit can put someone in jail for life!" I was getting angrier by the moment thinking about it.

"Your mind was somewhere else. Nobody could blame you. But you know what?"

"What?"

"I blame myself, actually."

"Why?" I quizzed.

"Because I wasn't there for you to turn to."

"Zelle—"

"Shit was so fucked up then," he continued, not hearing me call his name. "All I can say is I'm sorry you went through all that you did, and I'm sorry I didn't do my best to protect you. I love you. I know you won't ever forget your past, but none of that matters now because we got each other, and I ain't letting no harm come your way if I can help it."

"I love you, too, Zelle. Who needs Kayne anyway when I got you?" I smiled.

"It's nothing wrong with you loving him, Amina. No matter what nobody says, I'm a man and even I know it takes time for a heart to heal. When me and Tracy broke up, it tore me up. She was the only female I ever said 'I love you' to. It fucked me up when I found out she was smoking. I had no choice but to let her go. I tried to help her, but you can't force an addict to do shit. Once that shit takes over your body, it's over." He looked sad. I had never heard my brother open up about his relationship with her before.

"How is she doing now?"

"I ain't talked to her in about a month. She missed her last visit with Canoray."

"Poor baby, I know he was upset."

"Yeah, he was at first. I tried to tell him she was in the hospital and would see him soon. He ain't asked about her since. I'm dreading the day that he does, for real. Every child needs a mother."

"You know he's welcome to come stay over with me whenever. I need to spend some time with my lil' nephew anyway. Has he warmed up to Kelly yet?"

"Yeah, they're close. I just appreciate her being woman enough to take on the mommy role. It's crazy how I gave you and Kayne such a hard time, and now I'm with Kelly," he laughed.

"Pretty much!" I laughed, playfully rolling my eyes.

"To tell you the truth, you being away is what brought us together. I don't know if you know, but Kelly really missed you while you was away. When she wasn't able to visit you, she would always call me and check up on how you was doing. We ended up going out a few times, just as friends, and became closer as time went on. She was going through it with her man and things with me and Tracy were

slowly falling apart. Being there for each other turned into something good."

"I'm happy for you two," I told Zelle honestly. "I remember the day we were painting at the house, and Kelly had on them shorts trying to get your attention." We both fell out laughing. The rest of the meal, Zelle told me funny stories about Canoray. We laughed long after we were finished eating. It was the best time I'd had since my homecoming.

Chapter 5

Thursday—July 27, 2006

I couldn't take it anymore. After working with the fellas at The Shop, I was ready for a real job. My parole officer gave me a list of job postings to consider. I decided to go after the receptionist job at Blue Sky Independent Living Community. It started at twelve dollars an hour, and Kelly had managed to do some gangsta-ass research to find out that Marla worked there, too. During the interview, I was so nervous I had to force myself to sit still. I'd already told my P.O. that I really wanted the job, and even asked her to put in a good word for me with her close friend, Kathy Mimms, who was conducting the interview. As Kathy looked over my application, I realized that even with my P.O. and Kathy being friends, I would need a miracle to get her to hire a twenty-year-old black female with a criminal

record, a history of mental instability and a job history consisting of one job that lasted two weeks.

"I spoke with Mary. I actually know her from high school. We both graduated from McCauley. You've heard of that school, right?" she asked, putting on her glasses to take a better look at my application.

"Yeah, I heard it was a really good school." I smiled pleasantly as she looked at me directly. To my surprise, she smiled back.

"Back in high school I would've said the opposite. I hated being at an all-girl school, but hey, I turned out fine." She laughed. I made it a priority to laugh along. "Anyway, I could really use another receptionist in the main building. Are you looking for something full time?" I nodded. My nervousness wouldn't let me speak. Kathy removed her glasses, smiling again. Something about her was so sincere.

"Look, Amina. I can see that you're kind of nervous, and I completely understand why. But please don't be. I'm not here to judge you. Mary has informed me of your situation and also told me that you're a pretty bright girl. I understand you earned your high school diploma while you were away?"

"Yes."

"That's great, because a diploma or GED is required here."

I nodded again.

"Have you thought about college?"

"Yes, I'm considering a business degree at Cincinnati State."

"That's wonderful. We have a couple of girls working

here from Cincinnati State that you could probably talk to. When will you be able to start, and what shift are you looking for?"

"I can start as soon as possible, and I'd prefer day shift."

"Excellent! Our day shift is from eight a.m. to five p.m. daily. One weekend day is required, and you'll work from ten in the morning to seven at night. I can start you this coming Monday, which is the 31st. Another receptionist will work with you your entire first week, but after that the front desk will be all yours."

I nodded my confirmation.

"We start our receptionists off at twelve dollars an hour, and after ninety days you will be given a fifty-cent raise. Our dress code is black slacks or khakis, and a solid color shirt, preferably white or blue, but any color is fine. Capris are fine in the spring and summer and sandals with a heel, but absolutely no flip-flops or tennis shoes. Also, you'll be given a name badge that must be worn at all times while on the premises."

"Everything sounds great, and I'm excited to work here. So Monday at eight a.m.?" I confirmed.

"That's right." She smiled at me, feeling my enthusiasm. "Did you have any questions?"

"Well, actually, I was wondering if I could be called Mya instead of Amina. It's my middle name." That was a total lie. My middle name was Li'Auna, but if I was going to move on from my past and more importantly, get close to Marla, I had to use an alias.

"Absolutely, whatever makes you comfortable. Everything on this application is kept between you and me,

so think of this as a brand new start." She smiled.

"Thank you so much." I stood to shake her hand.

"Welcome to the staff. I'll see you on Monday to get you set up with Human Resources to fill out your new employee paperwork, then you'll go to Security for your badge. By that time, I should have you set up with your trainer."

"Thank you, Ms. Mimms, I really appreciate this."

"No problem. In the meantime, if you need anything before then don't hesitate to call my office. I'm here weekdays, eight to five thirty, and Saturdays, ten to seven. Off on Sundays." I noticed the navy blue WWJD bracelet on her wrist, and knew I had witnessed a miracle. Thank God she was a Christian.

* * * *

I used my last check from Mike to purchase some work clothes, but in order to carry out my plan, I had to give myself a whole new look. I decided to dye and straighten my hair. I went with jet black, which I got done at a beauty shop in Westwood. I went back to the hood to get my hair cut in a blunt Chinese cut with bangs by a chick named Carleeta. She worked out of her apartment, downtown on Elm, but the bitch was cold with a pair of scissors and could go hands up with any professional in the city. My shit looked good, and at first glance you would have mistaken me for another person. I went for my manicure and pedicure at the salon conveniently located on the sixth floor of my apartment building.

I spent Saturday and Sunday relaxing, trying to prepare

myself for what would really be my first professional job. Monday morning I woke up before my alarm clock, eager to start the day and my plan of attack. I skipped breakfast and sang Beyoncé's *"Ring the Alarm"* over and over again in my head the entire way to work. After leaving Human Resources and receiving my badge, I headed toward the main building, where I would be working. As I walked through the automatic double doors of Blue Sky, I smiled as I approached the front desk. Even if I hadn't already known what Marla looked like, I would have recognized her. She was huge, plus she had the glow of a woman in love and about to be married. Too bad I was going to rain on her parade.

Marla sat at the front desk sipping a Strawberries and Crème frappuccino from Starbucks while looking at a *"Good Housekeeping"* magazine. As I reached the desk I smelled Chanel No. 5 in the air. Marla looked up to see me setting my purse and keys down. She sighed like she'd just finished running a race and rubbed her belly. I was surprised to see her so soon, but definitely not disappointed. I scanned her face for flaws, only finding that her skin was somewhat oily. She wore heavy eyeliner which was unnecessary. If I had her hazels I wouldn't have even used eye makeup. Her teeth were pearly white with a small overbite.

"Hi, you must be Mya. I'm Marla." She extended her hand with a smile. "I'll be training you this week." I glanced down at her other hand, which she was still using to rub her belly, looking for proof, and there it was. The size of the rock on her finger was sickening. I promised myself that once I got Kayne back, I would make him buy me an even bigger diamond.

"Yup, I'm the new girl," I laughed, shaking her hand.

"Well, there's not too much to learn or do with this job. It's really easy. You should catch on quickly. I've been working the desk over in Special Needs for about four months now to stay off my feet, but I'm actually an RN." She motioned for me to come around to the back of the desk and stood up to grab me a chair. "I should be popping this big head lil' boy out soon enough."

"When are you due?" I asked, giving her my "how cute" smile.

"September 5th, but I'm praying he comes earlier than that."

"I bet you are," I said, looking at the size of her belly. "I don't have any kids but all my friends do. I think I'm about ready for one now." That was a lie.

"My fiancé begged me to have this one." As soon as those words came out her mouth I wanted to wring her neck. "At first I wasn't too sure, but then I figured I'm twenty-four, and I ain't getting no younger."

"I understand. You said you were having a boy. Is that what you wanted?"

"I really wanted a girl, but just as long as the baby is healthy, I'm happy."

"If I had a baby girl, we would be broke. I would shop more than I do now." We both laughed.

"Let me get you started on the computer and show you how to log into the system."

It only took an hour for her to school me on all the ins and outs of the job, then we were back to what Marla probably thought was casual conversation.

"So when's the wedding?" I asked cheerfully.

"Right now, we don't have a specific date. We were thinking about a spring wedding next year in May, but I'm too anxious to wait that long. I want a small outside wedding, probably in Eden Park, but if I move it up to the winter it would have to be inside a church."

"You taking his last name or are you gonna hyphenate yours?"

"Hyphenate?" Marla asked.

"You know, a lot of women are hyphenating their names and adding their husband's to the end."

"Oh no," Marla chuckled, "I'm definitely taking his. I'll be Mrs. Keon NaCore," she said proudly, trying out the name for size. "His first name is Keon but sometimes I call him Kayne. It's a little nickname I gave him years ago."

This bitch was straight up lying. Everyone knew Keon as Kayne. What was she stuntin' for? Not only did she have my man, but she was crazy.

"Mrs. Keon NaCore," I repeated for her benefit. "NaCore ... that's a name I've never heard before. Marla NaCore. That sounds nice."

"Yeah, I think so, too," she admitted, admiring her ring.

"A wedding in Eden Park would be pretty. You two must really be in love, look at you, you're glowing." I smiled, but on the inside, I was about to throw up.

"Yeah, that's my heart for real." She rubbed her belly and smiled. "We only been together two years, but I've known him for close to four. The crazy thing is, I actually proposed to him." She laughed with a big stupid grin on her

face. I tried to keep my look of surprise to a minimum, but inside, I was heated.

"Are you serious?"

"Yup, he came home from jail in December, and I was pregnant by January. I was with him the whole time he was locked up. I guess I just missed him so much, I couldn't wait for him to ask me first."

This was going to be easier than I thought. This bitch had no pride, and she was flat out dumb. If she was crazy enough to tell me something this pathetic the first day she met me, I was sure by the end of the week I would have the whole scoop.

"Was he surprised?"

"Girl, it took him two weeks to give me an answer. But as soon as he found out I was pregnant he said he was ready." This chick was really letting it all out.

"So you bought the ring and everything?"

"Yeah. I bought his and mine before he came home."

"Look at the size of that rock on your finger! Either you get paid good from here or he doing something right." I attempted to pry deeper.

Marla held out her hand, admiring her ring. "Girl, you think I got money for this? He just got a gold band, and I paid for that, but I financed mine." She smiled proudly. "What they say, three months' salary is what a man should spend on a diamond?" I shrugged my shoulders. Marla pulled out a pretend calculator and playfully punched numbers. "I think this is the equivalent to three months of what he makes." She laughed, and I did, too. "For real though, I knew he was fresh out and couldn't afford one, so I had my baby's back. But he's back on his feet again now. You know how niggas are. They bounce back faster than a basketball."

"True. Did you hook up while he was locked down?"

"We got serious in '04 when his so-called girl left him hanging. I started visiting and sending money. You know, just being there for him. I just hope we don't have to go through that again because it wasn't easy juggling school, work and his visits, making sure shit would be right when he got home."

I couldn't believe Kayne had told this girl I left him hanging. But if that wasn't full proof that he was just using her, the fact that *she* proposed to *him* and it took him two weeks to answer sure in hell was. Better yet, the fact that she had to buy her own ring was a sure sign that she didn't mean that much to him. Maybe my baby was missing me.

"You didn't talk before he got locked up?"

"We did, but nothing serious. I was concentrating on school and getting out of my crazy-ass cousin's house. I think if he'd had his way, we would have been together after we first met, but he didn't pressure me."

"Well, I guess you came at the perfect time, with his girl leaving him and all."

"They had only been together a few months, but they lived together before he went in. As soon as he fell that bitch was gone. You know how that goes," she said, rolling her eyes while flipping through a pregnancy magazine she had grabbed out of her purse earlier.

"Gold digger," I stated. She laughed in agreement.

At noon, I went out to pick us up some lunch and we

chatted even more as we ate our chicken salads.

"You haven't told me anything about yourself. No boyfriend?" she asked, giving me her full attention.

"Actually, I'm in the same situation you just got out of. My boyfriend is doing two years right now, and it's only been six months. It's getting harder for me day by day."

"I know the feeling girl, but stand by him. I'm telling you he will love you even more for it. How long y'all been together?"

"Six years," I said solemnly.

"Damn, y'all tight then. Time will fly by, just hang in there." Marla seemed at a loss for words. "Where you get your hair done at? I like that." She changed the subject.

"Urban Expressions."

"Westwood?"

"Yeah, I always go to the one out there. I only been to the one in Avondale once."

"I'ma have to check it out. Never been."

"You should, everybody in there is cold." I began bagging my trash to throw it out. The rest of the day the phone rang off the hook. People were calling about the annual picnic taking place that Saturday in the development's private park. Marla told me the funniest thing she had ever seen was a bunch of old people walking around eating hamburgers and hot dogs, some of them with their teeth falling out. I couldn't even imagine.

* * * *

After work, I stopped by my mom's. I had talked to her but

hadn't seen her in a week. I pulled into the driveway of her new house. After leaving her abusive ex-boyfriend, Markus, she found another job working for the city, making a little more change, which allowed her to finally buy her own home—a cute three bedroom with a basement and patio on a quiet suburban street. I was happy for my mother. She finally seemed content and was so proud of her house, which reminded me of a gingerbread house, with its plum-colored shutters and rounded front door. The colorful selection of flowers in the front yard added to the pleasant ambiance of her home.

Getting out of my car, I noticed a gray Corsica with tinted windows parked in front of the house next door. I knew an elderly lady lived there, but she didn't drive, and I had never noticed the car around before. It just seemed out of place. It was beat up with a huge dent in the passenger's side door, and the front hub cap was missing on the same side as the dent. Out of all my years of living in the hood, I had never seen a bucket with tinted windows, although I had to admit if I were the one driving that car I would have concealed my identity, too. The strange thing about it was that the car was running and was parked only about a foot away from my mother's driveway, and that was awfully close considering how much room there was.

I only glanced at the car, taking in its appearance quickly, but as I walked up the steps, I felt like there were eyes watching me. It didn't help that my mom took damn near ten minutes to get to the door. I had left my key to her house at home. I tried to dismiss the eerie situation as just another broke nigga checking out what he couldn't have

and stepped inside when she finally made it to the door with half of her hair curled and the rest unfinished.

"Where you getting ready to go?" I asked, following her to the bathroom.

"Gary's picking me up. We're going to check out that new seafood restaurant, Pappadeaux. They supposed to have really good food. I never been. Gary said they got the bomb crab legs, and you know me and my crab legs." She grinned excitedly into the bathroom mirror, finishing her hairstyle of spiral curls.

"Yeah, I heard about that place. Kelly told me it was really good." I stood in the doorway admiring what she was wearing. Silverish-gray gauchos, with a black backless halter and a pair of silver Gucci pumps that I had purchased for her as a late 39th birthday present.

"You know Gary knows all the hot spots in the city, especially restaurants. That man know he can eat." She giggled, running her fingers through her curls, then reached for her mascara.

"You looking good, Ma, so where you going after dinner?" I smiled.

"Thanks, baby, we'll probably meet his friend and his wife at Jazz in the Park for some drinks afterward. What you getting into tonight? You spending the night here?"

"No, I'm gonna go home. Just checking up." The doorbell rang. My mom quickly applied a coat of Mocha lip gloss and rushed to the door.

"There's chili I made last night in the fridge if you're hungry!" she called out as she opened the door for Gary. I headed to the kitchen to prepare a bowl to take home for dinner.

On my way out, I kissed my mother and greeted Gary, who was patiently waiting on the couch in his tan linen short set. I had to admit that I liked Gary, not only because he was practically rich, being the owner of six luxury car washes in Cincinnati and Columbus, but because he made my mother the happiest I had ever seen her. My mother had spent all of her time the past few years worrying about me and working with the lawyer she retained, who eventually uncovered the truth behind my arrest and the corrupt officers. I was relieved to finally see her stress free.

The first time I met Gary I knew he was cool; I didn't feel any funny vibes or get suspicious of him. He treated my mother like a queen. It also helped that the man looked good. He had green eyes, olive-colored skin and features that proved his Creole heritage. Since Markus, I had become extremely overprotective of my mother. It was a relief to know that with Gary, she was in good hands and could be the strong woman I always knew she could be.

"You two have fun, and take care of my momma, Gary," I said with a smile as I opened the front door to leave.

"You know I always do." He grinned, putting his arm around my mother's waist as she blushed like a little school girl.

"Okay, call me later, Ma." I closed the door behind me and immediately noticed the Corsica pulling away. I thought about mentioning it to Gary, but I didn't want to alarm him or my mother. Knowing how 'bout it he was, there was no doubt Gary would have walked right over and knocked on the window. When he and my mother started getting serious she told him all about Markus—from the fight between us and her kicking me out to him abusing her. Gary knew it all and he stayed. That's why my mother loved him so much, because he was still there even after hearing about all her drama.

He was also the one who had an alarm system installed in my mom's house and purchased a small handgun for her protection. My mother believed that living in the suburbs made her safe. Her new neighborhood was the complete opposite of Over the Rhine, but when you were dealing with a crazy person like Markus, nowhere was completely safe. Gary, being from the streets of New Orleans, knew this.

I hit the gas to catch up with the Corsica, which was almost a block ahead of me. That was the only day I was actually grateful for that ridiculously long light. I made a mental note of the license plate number and repeated it to myself over and over again until I came to another light and had time to jot it down. I started to follow the car, but thought better of it. I had the plates, and that was good enough.

Chapter 6

Saturday—August 5, 2006

It had just gotten dark outside. We were cleaning up after the annual picnic when Marla mentioned that Kayne would be picking her up and that she wanted me to meet him. I almost spilled the pan of baked beans I was carrying inside as soon as she said it. My mind began racing through all possible excuses to get away early, when I was suddenly saved by my cell. I picked up to hear Damen greeting me with a cheerful hello. As relief took over, I relaxed, set the beans down and walked away to talk to him in private.

Our conversation was brief. He was just calling to remind me that he and Shayna would be in town Sunday to visit with me and Zelle and to suggest that we go out to dinner at Palomino. I knew it was just to check up on me. Why else would he come in town just for one day? I returned to the cafeteria where Marla and a supervisor named Donna, who I absolutely could not stand, were packaging up the leftovers.

"Donna, I have an emergency. A friend of mine just had an accident and is being taken to the hospital. Is it okay if I go?" I put stress in my voice.

"Oh my goodness, will they be okay?" Marla commented in a shocked tone.

"I'm not sure. Her husband said it was really bad. The car was totaled, and she's unconscious."

"Yeah, of course you can go. I hope everything is alright."

"Thanks. I'll see you all later."

"Okay," Marla said as I left out in a hurry.

Pulling out, I saw Kayne pulling in and up to the front entrance. He was driving Marla's Lexus SUV. Luckily, he didn't notice me. I knew it would probably be a few minutes before Marla came out, so I pulled into the BP directly across the street. Not wanting to bring any suspicion on myself, I went in for a bottled water then sat in the car waiting for them to pull off. I knew I was taking a big risk of fucking up my game plan, but curiosity took over, and I couldn't control it. I followed them all the way to their apartment in the Fairfield Point apartments.

Although my job was in Fairfield, I had no idea that was where Marla lived. I pulled into a parking spot directly across from their front door, turned off the engine, cracked all the windows so I could eavesdrop and reclined my seat all the way back. I had a perfect view of them from my rearview mirror. Marla opened the door, and Kayne brushed past her entering first—something he never would have done to me. For some reason, he was angry. I recognized his body language. I figured maybe they had gotten into it earlier, but Marla paid it no mind as she followed him inside with her overly-cheerful ass. I had never seen a pregnant bitch so happy in all my days. I sat a few minutes longer, hoping to make out what they were doing inside by their shadows. In less than two minutes, Kayne was back out the door. Marla followed after him. Slouched in my driver's seat, I could now see them in my side mirror and could hear every word.

"Where the hell you going?" Marla grabbed the driver's side door as Kayne tried to close it.

"To handle my business, where you think?" He started the car.

"Nigga, am I supposed to sleep by myself again tonight?" She had both her hands on her big pregnant hips.

"Man, I ain't 'bout to argue with yo' silly ass all outside and shit. Go in the house. I'll be home when I get home." He sounded annoyed. I remembered whining to him about staying out all night when we lived together, but I couldn't remember him ever talking to me that way.

"What about the church? We were supposed to go look at that church in Walnut Hills tomorrow for the wedding." She sounded extremely upset. I was looking forward to a big blow out. Hearing Kayne talk to her like shit got my adrenaline going.

"What time?"

"Two o'clock. I told you earlier today."

"You gon' have to reschedule or go by yourself. Gotta

run to Kentucky in the morning and don't know what time I'll be back."

"What the fuck you mean? You told me yesterday you would go. How in the hell can you tell me to go by myself? Am I getting married to myself, nigga?! How am I supposed to even get there if you got my fuckin' car?" She was screaming now.

"I'll bring it back in the morning." He slammed the door and peeled off, leaving Marla with smoke coming out of her ears. As soon as I heard her front door slam, I called Kelly. Driving out of the parking lot, I headed toward home with a Kool-Aid smile spread across my face. Things would be a lot easier than I thought.

"What's good?" she answered.

"Guess where I'm coming from?"

"Where?"

"Kayne and Marla's house. I followed them home."

"What? Did they see you?"

"Hell no, I followed them home from work. They just had a huge blowout about Kayne leaving to go out of town. She's all pissed because they were supposed to go look at a church for the wedding."

"Are you serious? So he just blew her off like that?"

"Girl, yes, and took her car," I laughed.

"Dang!" She laughed as well. "Hey, I know who we can find out some shit about Marla and Shalauna from."

"Who?"

"Butter, I saw her crazy ass last night downtown. She was catching the bus, so I gave her my number to call me. I told her we need to talk."

Andrea "Butter" Malone was a beautiful hustler's wife turned crack head. Kelly and I had known Butter since we were kids, and at one point, we both looked up to her. Butter was only thirty, but was so gone on the pipe she could pass for fifty. She got her name from being one of the most beautiful light-skinned women to ever walk the earth. Her skin was smooth and yellow, and her naturally gold tinted hair ran directly down her back at least sixteen inches. No matter how hot it was, you could always catch Butter with her hair down her back. It was her pride and joy, and was what made her feel beautiful. You could always find her on a corner somewhere downtown rocking something short with heels and the gold cross necklace that her husband, Rome, gave her in '92. I never saw Butter without that chain around her neck. It must have been the only part of her past that she still had left.

Surprisingly, no one ever had the nerve to try to steal it from her. It had to be worth a good meal ticket, but even on her worst day, I knew Butter had too much pride to let it go. Butter was a hustler herself and respected by all the dope boys in the hood. She was the wife of the eighties Cincinnati legend, Rome. Rome was incarcerated in '98 on one of the heaviest drug charges you could get. You might as well have said Rome was serving life, so his wife and pride and joy was left heartbroken.

It wasn't the lack of money that drew Butter to the pipe. No, Rome's empire was so large, Butter had money to last her probably the rest of her life. It was the pain of being without Rome, who had taken care of her and loved her since she was only fifteen and he was twenty-two. They

never had the chance to have any children, which only made their forced separation worse.

I remember Butter once telling me that she tried her hardest to hold on and be strong for Rome, but lonely nights and days caught up. She told me the first time she hit the pipe felt like when Rome took her virginity. She said it felt so good that she couldn't let go, just like she couldn't let go of him. But I knew the people around Butter had a lot to do with her downfall. They were all waiting to see her crumble, waiting to see the day when she didn't have a dime left. Her friends, and even her own family, envied Butter and wanted nothing more than to see her become what they already were—broke and lonely. After all, misery loves company. I knew we had a lot in common, and although I admired her, I never wanted to fall that hard.

"Cool, call me as soon as you hear from her."

"I will. You're going to dinner tomorrow, right?" asked Kelly.

"Yeah, I'll be there. We'll talk."

Chapter 7

Sunday—August 6, 2006

Our reservation at Palomino downtown was for seven thirty p.m., but of course I arrived fifteen minutes late just to make an entrance. Damen, Shayna, Zelle and Kelly were already seated at a big table in the back. As soon as I walked in I could see Shayna flagging me down. I could tell she was excited to see me. I felt the same about seeing her and Damen. I missed him so much I could have cried when he hugged me, but I held it together like the stronger woman I had become.

After ordering a light appetizer, Kelly and I both excused ourselves to the ladies' room.

"Girl, can you please talk to your brother? He been tripping ever since we ran into Shawn at a gas station the other night," Kelly said as we both stood in front of the mirror

touching up our makeup.

"What? I never thought of him as the jealous type, but I'll talk to him as long as you ain't fucking Shawn." I smirked.

"Girl, please! You remember how that nigga tried to play me. Let's face it, the nigga is broke now that he took a L. I ain't got time for him. Old news, straight up," she said with a roll of her eyes.

"Just making sure. So what did Butter say? You talked to her, right?"

"She was just telling me that she knows who Shalauna and Marla are. She used to cop from Shalauna sometimes with some white chick she knew named Michelle. She said she could find out where Shalauna is just in case you ever need to know. She didn't say much about Marla."

"Well, I'll keep that tip in my back pocket. Tell her I might be calling her sooner rather than later." I wanted to get Shalauna's snitching ass just as much as Marla.

"Girl, you know you crazy. How much shit can you fit up your sleeve?"

"I'm still trying to figure that out." We both laughed as we left the restroom. Entering the dining room again, the very first thing I noticed was a couple who seemed to be so wrapped up into each other they didn't know the rest of the world existed. Their faces were so close together I had to do a double take to realize the woman was Marla. For a split second I panicked until I realized the guy she was with was not Kayne. Bells went off in my head as my new plan began to surface. I was stuck in my tracks with a Grinch smile glued to my face.

"Girl, what's wrong with you?" Kelly asked in confusion.

"Do you see what I see?" I quizzed in a satisfied tone.

"What?" Kelly looked even more puzzled.

"Over there." I pointed slyly. "That's Mrs. Keon NaCore."

"That's Marla?" she asked in disbelief.

"Yeah, that's her, but is that Kayne?" I couldn't hide the sarcasm.

"Hell no, it ain't! Damn, she cheating with that lame?"

I scoped out the guy as much as I could from the view point, and brothaman was definitely looking like his pockets were kind of low. No watch, no chain, nothing that said money. He wore a plain gray button down shirt with black dress pants. I couldn't make out his shoes. His complexion was like coffee with milk. He rocked a goatee and bald head, which topped off his corny look. He even went so far as to have a silver hoop earring in his left ear. Yes, a hoop! Not a diamond stud, but a hoop. Marla was looking like she had landed God's gift to women. All I could make out was the extreme tightness of the black sleeveless dress she was wearing. It was obvious she felt sexy when she put it on, but I had to question if it was maternity or out of her *before I got pregnant* collection. I watched as he seductively fed her a shrimp.

"Damn, what's wrong with this lame bitch? She got Kayne and risking him for this?" Kelly still couldn't believe her eyes.

"I gotta get my baby back for real now. This bitch is just downright ungrateful." I shook my head in complete shock as I watched him continue to feed her, while Marla pretended the shrimp was the best thing she'd ever tasted.

"Girl, you damn right," Kelly agreed while rummaging through her huge Chanel bag, finally pulling out her tiny digital camera. "We gotta get a flick of this shit. It'll come in handy later." I wanted to jump up and down with excitement. A picture was something that hadn't even crossed my mind. As Kelly quickly snapped a few shots of the loving couple, I anticipated what I would say when I walked over.

"You going over there?" Kelly asked with excitement in her voice.

"Hell yeah, but I'm just gonna play it cool. She don't think I know who Kayne is, so I wanna see what she'll say."

"Alright, I'm going back to the table. You shouldn't let her meet me just in case I need to play spy later."

"Right." I casually approached the table, glad neither one of them noticed which direction I came from.

"Hey, Marla!" I greeted her with a smile.

"Oh my goodness. Hey, girl!" She was completely caught off-guard and I could see her nervousness rising. "Who are you here with?" she asked.

"Just some friends. I noticed you over here and felt kind of bad because I didn't get to meet your fiancé at the picnic. Hi, I'm Mya, I work with Marla. She talks about you all the time." I extended my hand to her date who looked absolutely pissed that I had mistaken him for someone else, but shook my hand anyway. Marla sat speechless. So I spoke for her.

"So have you guys decided on the date yet?" The guy shifted in his seat, showing his frustration.

"Excuse me for a minute." He got up and headed to the

men's room. Marla looked about ready to cry.

"I'm sorry," I said as apologetically as I could. "Is this a bad time?"

"Is it okay if we talk Monday?"

"Sure, I didn't mean to cause any—"

"Oh no, it's okay. We'll talk." She cut me off. I knew from her tone that she was going to spill the beans to me tomorrow with no shame. I couldn't understand why she didn't just lie, but then again, she wasn't gangsta enough to play it off like I would have.

I returned to the table and Kelly gave me a wink. Damen poured me a glass of the wine he had ordered. I smiled inside and out as we all made a toast to happiness.

Chapter 8

Monday—August 7, 2006

"Now for an update on the shooting in Avondale. Police have identified the victim as forty-two-year-old Gary Ridges. The owner of the popular car wash bearing his name, Ridges was shot twice in the arm and leg at four thirty a.m. in front of his Avondale home. Authorities believe the motive might have been robbery. Ridges is listed in critical condition at an undisclosed location. Witnesses say the gunman fled the scene in a gray Corsica and identified him as a black male, around 5'11", between the age of forty and forty-five, wearing all black. Police are currently looking for more information and are encouraging witnesses to call Crime Stoppers at —"

I muted the TV and lay across the bed in shock. The first thing I thought was that this was all my fault. If I would have just told Gary about the suspicious car instead of trying to play Sherlock, this never would have happened. Before I broke down in tears, I stopped and remembered that Gary was still alive. "Thank you, God," I said aloud. The ringing phone startled me.

"Amina?" My mother was bawling on the other end.

"Ma, I just heard on the news. Where are you? I'm on my way."

"I'm at the hospital," she said, still in tears. It took me ten minutes to calm her down enough to tell me exactly what happened. Gary was shot as he walked up to his house after dropping my mom off. I was so relieved that my mother wasn't hurt. After calling off from work for the day, I rushed to the hospital. The entire drive, I kept having flashbacks of the Corsica sitting in front of the house. Who would do a thing like this? It only took a half of a second to come to an answer: Markus. I didn't want to tell my mother I knew about the car all along and didn't say anything, but I felt like I owed it to her and to Gary. Besides, whoever pulled this stunt could be out to get her next. She would have to come stay with me until this was solved. There was absolutely no other option.

Walking into the hospital, I prepared myself to see my mother a nervous wreck. My heart was beating a thousand times a second, and all I felt was guilt. I hugged her and she broke down in my arms.

"How is he?" I asked as soon as she pulled herself together enough to answer me.

"I don't know yet. I'm waiting on the doctor to talk to me. Come to the waiting room with me and Gary's moth-

er."

"Ma, wait." I hesitated for a second. "Do you have any idea who might have done this?"

"No, baby, but when Gary's conscious the police will get information from him so we can find out."

"Mom, I got to tell you something." Tears welled up in my eyes.

"What is it?" Her eyes looked sad and exhausted like she'd been up for hours.

"Before you left Thursday night, I noticed a gray Corsica in front of the house. I knew something wasn't right, and I was going to say something, but I just didn't want to ruin your night. Mommy, I'm so sorry!" I was crying so she embraced me and hushed me until I stopped.

"Baby, I know you are." She smoothed my hair. "Shhh ..." she whispered into my ear, "he's going to be alright." I was so relieved that she wasn't mad at me, but I still felt awful. Then suddenly I remembered I had the plates from the car and felt a twinge of hope.

"Wait, I got the license plate, I wrote it down." I rummaged through my purse, looking for the small receipt I had jotted the license plate number on. "I was going to call Gary and give it to him. I just didn't want to scare you, that's why I didn't bring it up." After digging through keys, makeup, my cell phone and tons of other junk, I finally lucked up on it. "Here you go," I handed it to her. "Give it to the police."

"Thank you so much, baby." She hugged me tightly. "They may want to speak to you. You count as a witness."

"If they need to speak to me that's fine," I assured her,

dismissing the fact that I hated coming in contact with any police since my case. I couldn't be selfish at a time like this.

We went into the waiting area, and she introduced me to Gary's mother, Gwen. She was a really sweet lady. We talked for a while, and she told us about her experience with Hurricane Katrina. Her home of thirty-five years had been ruined in the hurricane, so she came to Cincinnati to live with her only child, Gary. Her story was so sad, I silently said a prayer for her as we sat there waiting to hear from the doctor. I prayed that God would keep Gary alive, if not for my mother, for his.

I stayed at the hospital until ten that night, waiting to hear the results of all the tests they were running. Overall the results were good and gave us all hope that Gary would survive; however, he was still unconscious. The doctors allowed all three of us to visit with him for thirty minutes around six o'clock. Gwen sat with him for fifteen minutes; she gave my mother the last fifteen. I went in with her as she sat there and talked to him. While I listened to her speak to him, I couldn't help but think of Kayne. I wished I could hold his hand and pour out all my feelings to him that way.

The doctors were only allowing one person to stay the night. Gwen stayed. I called Zelle and had him meet us at my mother's house so she could pick up some clothes to stay with me until things cleared up. I knew it wasn't safe for the two of us to go alone.

When we finally got to my place, I ran my mom a hot bubble bath and changed the sheets on my bed so she could sleep with me. I set the alarm clock two hours early.

I knew she would want me to drop her off at the hospital on my way to work. We had already decided it wasn't safe for her to drive alone, day or night.

* * * *

"Girl, I got to let you in on a little secret. I know you was wondering what the hell that shit was about Sunday." Marla and I were sitting at her favorite lunchtime restaurant. She was treating to make up for her rudeness when I rolled up on her and her dude the day before.

"What is it?" I played confused and innocent.

"Well, dude I was with wasn't exactly my fiancé." Her eyes were big while she waited for my response.

"Oh, what's up with that?" I asked, surprised.

"Girl, it's kind of complicated. I've been seeing Jason, that's who you met, since before I met Keon. But we broke up for a couple of years because he was in the Navy and was stationed in Germany for a while." That explained the bald head.

"So, Keon doesn't know about him at all?"

"Girl, naw!" She had a perplexed expression on her face. "I mean, he ain't exactly the jealous type, but he wouldn't fuck with me if he knew I was tipping out on him like I been doing the last few months."

"Why'd you start?" I really wanted to know if there was another chick somewhere I needed to get rid of along with her stupid ass, but I'd let her spill the beans.

"I don't know. It just kind of happened. We had kind of a one night stand before Keon got out, and three months

later I saw him in the club and things heated back up. We been fucking around ever since. The thing is, I still want to marry Keon. I just don't know how to break it off with Jason. I think he's getting a little too used to this. After I get married, I want it to stop. I just don't know if he can handle that."

"Jason knows about Keon, right? I didn't get you in any trouble, did I?"

"Oh, girl, believe me, he knows. That's all he talks about. 'When you gonna leave Keon?'" she mocked in a deep voice. "See, Jason thinks the baby is his, 'cause we did it like a week before Keon came home, so I don't know whose it is to be honest. This shit is eating me up though. I feel like I need to break it off with Jason or come clean with Keon. The only thing is, I don't know if he's cheating, too, and if he is, I'll feel stupid for telling him, when I know damn well he ain't about to admit to shit he did. You feel me?"

"True, but have you had any reason to think he is?" I pressed again.

"I don't know, he just been acting real distant ever since I started planning this wedding. I don't know if I'm overwhelming him with all the decision making or if he just ain't ready. But one thing I have noticed is he been comparing me to his ex."

"What?" I exclaimed. "That's wrong!"

"Girl, yeah! Like when we argue or I bitch about something he'll tell me shit like, 'My girl ain't never used to bug me like this,' or, 'My baby ain't never used to bitch all the time about nothing.' Girl, that shit pisses me off so bad. I

mean, I'm pregnant, what the fuck do he expect?"

I nodded in agreement, beaming inside.

"I don't know if the old bitch is back in the picture and he's fucking her on the side, but I do know when it counted, that bitch wasn't there. *I* was there to see his ass every visitation." She pointed to herself. "*I* even took off work twice to make it to see him. *I* was the one putting money on his books, sending him letters, pictures, accepting his damn phone calls." She was getting worked up.

"So, you sure he didn't have both of y'all doing the same shit for him? Niggas is good for it."

"Hell no, because he always called begging me to come see him or send him money, 'cause no one else would. He would dog that bitch out, talking 'bout how she left him hanging and how much he hated her and wanted to kill her. Then as soon as we have a damn argument, he talking about that ho like she was a fucking angel. Shit pisses me off every time I think about it. He's either fucking her or some other ho he met. He's usually home, but it's always those nights at least once a week he don't come home, claiming he in the streets making money all night, but that's what every nigga out here say. I been bugging his ass about getting off the streets anyway. I ain't 'bout to marry no nigga who could be gone tomorrow and end up stuck alone with a baby."

"I feel you." She had a point. "You sure the girl who left him and the chick he comparing you to is the same chick?"

"I'm sure, 'cause besides me, she's the only other female he ever been in a relationship long enough with to call 'his girl.'"

"You know her name?"

"Nope, every time I asked he always acted like it was some big-ass secret. 'That shit is irrelevant,' is what he always used to say. Never seen the bitch either, and don't really care to," she said, eliminating my next question.

"Well, if you really love him and think you can work shit out, you should break it off with Jason. Then find out what's going on with Keon." I told her exactly what I knew she wanted to hear. "And if I were you, I would ask that nigga straight up if he trying to marry me or not, and if not, keep the shit moving. Too many out here to be tripping over one, no matter how in love you may be."

"You right. I will try to talk to him, get in his head a little bit. That is, if he'll let me."

"Damn, we better be getting back," I told her after glancing at my watch.

"Yeah, let's get out of here," she confirmed after looking at her own watch. "Thanks for the advice, and I'm hoping this conversation stays between us." She raised an eyebrow.

"Girl, of course. Matter of fact, it stays right here in Panera Bread. You know how nosy white folks is. We can't talk about this shit at work." We both laughed as we emptied our trays and walked to the car. In her mind, Marla and I were best friends. In my mind, I deserved an Oscar.

Chapter 9

Friday—August 25, 2006

"Hey, girl, I'm on my way to Penn Station to pick up some lunch. You want anything?" I stood over Marla, who looked like she was ready to burst.

"No, I'm getting off at three today. I can't believe today is my last day. I'll be gone for six weeks. You gonna be able to make it without seeing me every day?" she joked. "I know you gonna miss me."

"Oh yeah! I forgot you were leaving!"

"Some friend you are!" She rested her arms on her belly. "Mess around, and I won't come back."

"Well, you know I'll be at the hospital. I'm excited for you! Are you scared?"

"Girl, more scared about this baby daddy situation than anything."

"Marla, don't stress yourself, just be happy Keon doesn't suspect anything."

"You're right." She rubbed her belly.

"Are things any better between you two?"

"Yeah ... since we put the wedding on hold."

"On hold?" I was shocked to hear that.

"Yeah. We decided to wait until the baby turns one." She sounded and looked disappointed.

"Well, it could be for the best. It'll give you time to relax after having the baby and clear the whole situation with Jason. A year from now, girl, you'll be ready. You don't need too much on your shoulders anyway. A wedding is a big deal, and I know you want it to be perfect."

She smiled emotionally and then started to cry. Just an inch of me felt bad. "Yeah, you're right. I guess I was just in such a rush because I was scared that he would run away from me. You just don't understand how much I love him. I love him more than Jason. I mean, things are just different with Keon. I never been with nobody like him. I just want us to work."

Tell me about it, I thought as I went around the desk to hand her a tissue and give her a comforting hug.

"Marla, don't cry. Things will work out. They will, just let it go and don't hold on so tight." She nodded her head, drying her pathetic tears. "Now you sure you don't want anything, sweetie?"

"No, no, I'm sure. I'm not even hungry for a change." We both laughed, lightening the mood.

"Okay. Well, why don't you take a little break, walk around and get that baby ready to come out." I smiled.

"Yeah, I think I'll walk down and get some water."

* * * *

My heart was skipping beats as I walked out the door. I literally had my fingers crossed, hoping things would go smoothly. As I pulled up in the parking lot of Marla's apartment complex, I looked at the envelope addressed to Keon NaCore from a false Kentucky address. Inside were the four pictures of Marla and Jason at Palomino that Kelly had captured perfectly. I prayed that Marla wasn't the type to open Kayne's mail. I figured if she found it and saw the return address being from Kentucky she might think it was the other woman she already suspected he was going to see whenever he headed there.

All my worries were put to rest when I saw a black on black Dodge Charger pull in front of the apartment. Out stepped Kayne looking better than ever in a pair of crisp Red Monkey jeans, a clean button down shirt and a pair of Bathing Apes. His hair was freshly tapered, and I could tell just by looking at him that he smelled good. He hit the car alarm, and I heard it chirp, letting me know there was no one else with him. The pitch black windows could have deceived me though. Regardless, as soon as the front door was shut, I made a quick dash for the mailbox, which was right next to the front door of the townhouse. I dropped it in, nigger knocked and ran back to my car. I started the car and headed for Penn Station to pick up a drink just to make things seem normal. I hoped Kayne would call Marla at work to confront her, even though I highly doubted it. It

wasn't his style. He was more likely to try to catch her red handed if he even cared enough to try. I could have just mailed the envelope with the pictures, but I guess I just needed the thrill and assurance that it got there with no problem.

Twenty minutes later, I stopped at Marla's desk on the way back to mine.

"Feeling better?"

"Yeah, I think I'm actually going to be leaving in a few. Donna's letting me go early."

"Call me later so we can make a dinner date before you go into the hospital." I tried to read her face for any type of distress. I saw none. "Give me a hug before you go."

She stood up and gave me the kind of hug you give someone you trust.

"You know I will. Thanks for listening and giving me advice. I really needed someone real to talk to. You can't count on everybody, you know how that goes."

"Yeah, I know." Obviously she had no concept of what was real and what was fake. "But girl, let me get back to this desk before Donna's fat ass come out here looking for me." We both laughed as I walked away feeling proud of a job well done.

When I got to my desk, I began to ask myself why I was even going through all of this. I knew I could snatch Kayne back from Marla's weak ass without a thought. But here I was plotting and scheming to get what was rightfully mine. I guess in the beginning I counted her as my competition. That was before I realized she was no competition at all. Kayne didn't love her. It was plain for anyone to see. But

the real question was, did he ever really love me?

* * * *

After work I went home to change and pick up my mother for dinner. We had both been extremely stressed since the shooting and neither one of us was up to cooking. I decided on Benihana, thinking it would lift our spirits a little. I knew this would be the last evening me and my mother would spend together for a while. Gary was leaving the hospital the next morning, and she wasn't going to let him out of her sight.

"Ma, I really just want to tell you how sorry I am for everything that happened to Gary. I know I could have prevented it. I'm so sorry."

"Amina, I told you this was not your fault." She wiped away the tears that fell from my eyes with her dinner napkin. "Matter of fact, I blame myself. I was the one who let Markus into our lives."

"Mom, you can't blame yourself for his crazy ass doing what he did." I was getting pissed off just thinking about him.

"Baby, let me finish." Her soft tone calmed me. I saw a look in her eyes I had never seen before, one I can't even describe.

"I never told you the truth about some things, and I want to tell you now. When I first met Markus, he was a lawyer at that sad excuse of a law firm, as you already know. Even though he was a shady lawyer, he had a good share of money and was actually doing well for someone who start-

ed out on his own. He mostly dealt with injuries though. He had actually expressed a lot of interest in me since I started working there, but he was always charming, never disrespectful or pushy. I later found out that he was married. He didn't have any children, but he had been married to his wife for seven years and was married the whole time I was with him.

"After you got the letter from Damen, I decided to give him a chance. I didn't need old feelings coming back up, you know." I nodded. "I knew your father coming back around wasn't about me, but you, and that's why I needed something else to lean on and another relationship with a married man was the closest thing within reach. Every time I think about it, I get upset with myself for letting things go as far as they did with me and Markus, and most of all choosing him over you. To this day, I'm still ashamed of how I let you out of my life. I try to block the night you left out of my mind, but it's hard. Even after all these years, I can't seem to forgive myself. I was deeply depressed while he and I lived in Texas. I was literally sick for almost a whole year, even after I got away from him. I just thank God every day that he brought us back together."

"Why are you telling me this now, Ma?" I asked with tears in my eyes.

"I've always felt like I've owed you an explanation, and I needed to tell you this. I was just waiting on the right time to give it to you. I love you more than anything in this whole entire world. I know there have been times that it hasn't seemed like it, but I admit I've had some issues over the years that needed to be dealt with.

"While you were away I made a promise to get myself together for you. That's why I found a new job and bought a house. I wanted more than anything for you to be proud of me, to see me strong for once. I'm healed now. I feel like I can finally be the mother I always wanted to be. I'm not desperate for love anymore. When Damen left me before you were born, I went on a quest for love and put some of the most important things second. That's why I ended up involved with Tony, who didn't love me either. I'm over that now. I don't need a man's love to be able to live with myself. I love myself enough to do without a man. I love Gary and still have dreams of getting married one day, but if Gary decided to leave me tomorrow, I would be okay. I would be hurt, but I would still be breathing. I used to feel dead without a man there to say he loved me, and that's all I ever had was a man who *said* he loved me, never mind if he meant it or not. I was addicted to those three little words.

"I'm just thankful to God that I never had a drug or alcohol addiction, things could have been even worse. But most of all, what I want to say is that I hope you find happiness whether you're married or single, or just dating. But I don't want you to lose your morals just to gain that happiness, Amina. Never break up a home, because when you finally find a home of your own, someone will be outside the door waiting to break up what you took years to build. It's not worth all of that. Don't be like me, have love for yourself before you have love for any man. No one can love you more than you. Remember that, baby, if you don't remember anything else I've ever said, remember that."

I soaked in every word. "I love you, Mom, and I'm very

proud of you. You just made some mistakes like we all do. But you made sure I was taken care of. I never went without. I had friends whose moms were prostitutes or crack heads. You never gave me any reason to be ashamed of you or hate you, even after Markus, and I'm grateful for that."

"I love you, too, and I'm sorry for all the things I missed out on while my head was in the clouds."

"Mommy, we got plenty of time to catch up." I poured us both a glass of the wine we had ordered. "Let's make a toast." We both lifted our glasses.

"A toast to starting over," she said.

Chapter 10

Friday night—August 25, 2006

After helping my mother pack all of her belongings to go to Gary's house, I cleaned up to get ready for Canoray, who would be spending the night with me. I was so excited about being able to spend some one-on-one time with my nephew for the first time that I went to the store to get all kinds of snacks and kids' movies to watch.

"Hi, MiMi!" Canoray exclaimed as he and Zelle walked through the door.

"Hey, sweetie, what have you been up to?" I asked, picking him up for a hug.

"With daddy."

"With daddy? Did you go to the barber shop and get your hair cut? It looks nice."

"Yes." He looked shyly at Zelle. The boy was a spitting

image of his father.

"You're a big boy, huh? I got some movies to watch, do you like *'Spider-Man'*?"

"Yeah!"

"Okay, well, I have *'Spider-Man 2'*, *'Madagascar'*, and *'102 Dalmatians.'*" Those were some of the movies Zelle told me he had never seen.

"I want to watch them all, MiMi!"

"We will. Did you eat yet?"

"Yes, chicken nuggets."

"Well, let's put *'Spider-Man 2'* in. Can you be a big boy and watch it while Auntie talks to your daddy?" I asked, putting the movie in the DVD player.

"Yep!"

After getting him settled on the floor with cookies and milk, Zelle and I headed for the kitchen where I mixed us some drinks.

"Where's Kelly? I haven't talked to her today."

"She won't get off until eleven tonight. She's supposedly working somebody else's shift." Kelly worked for Time Warner Cable.

"Supposedly? What's up with that?"

"I don't know." He shook his head.

"What's going on with you two? Everything alright?"

"Yeah, we cool. I just been stressing about the business. Niggas been playing about booth rent. I'm about ready to let all my barbers go and shut that shit all the way down, maybe open up a liquor store or strip club or something."

"Kelly ain't having that, I can tell you that right now. But I thought everything was going good. You worked so

hard to get it up and going. You sure you just want to let it all go? Why don't you just find new barbers?"

"Yeah, that's what I'll have to do. I guess this shit just comes with the territory though. Damen told me that when I first started talking about getting a shop back in '02. Everything was good at first, but people always have to test you," he said. "They like to try to make their problems yours. Almost all my barbers are out there getting females pregnant and keep getting hit up for child support or abortion money. Then they think they can come up short on my money. But you're right, it took me years to be able to get my money right to get the shop. I just don't know about opening the new location, at least not until I make some replacements."

"Well, I know everything will work out. I'm just so happy to see you handling your business the legal way. I'm proud of you, for real."

"Shit, I'm proud of me, too! Getting legal ain't as easy as everybody thinks. You really got to go about it the right way or somebody will be waiting to fuck with you. Luckily, Damen had done it before me and already had connects who could clean me up real good so the shop could be in my name. If it wasn't for him I don't know if I could have pulled it off."

"I know. So is everything else going okay?"

"Everything else like what?" He looked at me suspiciously.

"Well, Kelly said something to me about you suspecting her of cheating with Shawn."

"Oh really? Well, if she is you can let her know it's her

loss because the nigga can't take care of her at all."

"Zelle, do you really think Kelly would do something like that? For one, Shawn hurt her in the worst way. He got three different girls pregnant while they were together. I can tell you no woman is going to give up a man like you to go back to that!"

"I know, and I don't really think shit is going on. I just been taking my frustration out on her lately. I don't know why. To make it up to her I'm going to get us tickets to Jamaica. I need a vacation anyway. It should be good for the both of us."

"I know she'll love that." I was happy that I had gotten to the bottom of that.

"How's work?" he asked, finishing the last of his drink.

"It's good. I like it because it's easy."

"Have you talked to Kayne?" He caught me off-guard.

"Nope, have you?"

"He came in the shop the other day. He asked how you were doing. I told him you was doing real good. I think he expected me to give him your number or something, but he didn't ask, and I wouldn't have given it to him anyway." Zelle had no idea he had just brightened my day.

"We'll probably run into each other sooner or later. I'm not in any rush to see him to be honest." I shrugged nonchalantly.

"I know, and you shouldn't be. I'm about to go. I need to stop back at the shop and make sure these niggas locked everything up right. I'll call you in the morning." After giving Canoray a hug, Zelle left and we watched movies until Canoray was knocked out cold on the living room couch. I

carried him carefully to my bed where he slept with me. The thought of Kayne wondering about me made for a peaceful night's sleep.

Chapter 11

Saturday—August 26, 2006

I was dressed in my best since Kelly and I had decided to go out. I had actually been feeling really shitty ever since I delivered the pictures to Kayne. Knowing that Kayne was thinking about me had lifted my spirits for only a short while. My mother's advice about breaking up a home played over and over in my head. Even though I knew I was probably doing Marla a favor, I still felt bad. I threw salt in the game when I could have just played fair. I knew when I did finally get to Kayne I didn't want him to know I sent the pictures. I was sure it would turn him off.

Beyoncé's *"Ring the Alarm"* came on the radio, lifting my spirits. Walking toward the club line, I had the perspective that I was doing right again. I planned to let loose and find me somebody to go home with. A one night stand

was just what I needed.

Two minutes in the club and niggas were literally flocking me and Kelly. If they weren't buying drinks, we weren't wasting time. Thirty whole minutes passed before someone finally offered to buy me a drink. Kelly was standing right next to me, so I told him my friend was drinking, too. After ordering two bottles of Belvedere, one for him and his boy, and one for me and Kelly, we all sat down together. We chatted as much as we could over the loud music. His name was Chris, he was twenty-six and doing his thing, obviously. The chemistry between us was strong. He turned me on the same exact way Kayne did. His whole style was grown man and very sexy. *Kayne might have some competition,* I thought as I watched Chris talking on his phone. It was hard for him to make out what the person on the other end was saying. He hung up and motioned for his friend, who was sitting next to Kelly, to come over.

"Yo, I think he said the club hit capacity. They going back to the telly," Chris said.

"We trying to chill or we out?" his friend replied, who was as cute as Chris.

"Shit, we can go, but I ain't trying to leave shorty over here," I heard him say. "She teasing me in those lil'-ass shorts." He looked me dead in the eyes and ran his hand up my thigh. I'd only had one fling since I had been home, and it was some straight bullshit. I was ready to open up for him right there in the club. I was so horny. "What's up? You trying to hit the telly?" He asked, pulling me closer and sucking on my neck just enough to make me say yes.

I looked over at Kelly, who I knew couldn't drive home alone. Even back in the day she never could fulfill her duty as designated driver when it was her turn.

"Yeah, I'll go, but let me talk to my girl real quick." I walked over to Kelly, who was sitting with cutie again. They didn't seem as interested in each other as me and Chris were. Kelly's mind seemed to be on Zelle. I let her know what was up and that I was driving her home whether she wanted me to or not. I'd only had two drinks so far. Chris and his friend, Mike, followed behind us.

Afterward I rode shotgun next to Chris in his all black Impala on twenty-sixes. Mike sat in the back rolling up some hydro that I wished I could hit.

"Why you so quiet, baby? You okay?" Chris asked.

"Yeah, I'm cool. What hotel we going to?"

"Hyatt, downtown. Three more of my niggas there but two of them got they chicks, so you won't be the only female, baby," he said, succeeding at making me feel more comfortable. "I got my own suite, so we'll have privacy. Is that alright with you?"

"Yeah, I'm glad to hear that." I gave him my sexy smile. "So y'all always hang at hotels?" I smirked.

"Not really, two of my niggas from Kentucky is up here so me, Mike and my other nigga stayed at the telly, too."

"Oh, okay. I got you." I wondered if all his friends looked as good as he did. Ten minutes passed and we were pulling up to the valet. I was starting to feel fucked up from the drink I was sipping while I rode, so I decided to take my six-inch stilettos off to spare myself any embarrassment.

"You want me to carry them shoes for you, baby?" Chris asked, helping me out of the car.

"I got them. Thanks." When we got to the elevator, Chris couldn't keep his hands off my ass. The elevator wasn't moving fast enough for me. We finally made it to the tenth floor and entered a room full of smoke. There were niggas everywhere, at least six, not including Chris and Mike. There were three girls sitting on laps. They said hi to me and Chris as he led me over to the table that held more liquor than the bar downstairs.

"You want another drink or you straight, shorty?"

"Naw, baby, I'm cool." I watched him pour a glass of straight Hennessy.

"Come on, let's go to my room." He took my hand and led me to the door, which seemed extremely far away with all the smoke. When he opened the door I almost pissed on myself when I realized who was standing on the other side. I let go of Chris' hand, standing in complete shock. I heard Chris' voice saying something, but I couldn't make out his words over the loud sound of my heart pounding ridiculously fast.

Kayne stared at me the same way I stared at him.

"Yo, y'all two know each other or something?" I heard Chris ask, but I still couldn't move.

"Yeah," Kayne replied, not all the way there either.

"My bad, nigga. It was nice meeting you, shorty. Ain't know you fucked with my boy."

"It's a long story," I managed to reply.

"You remember. I told you 'bout my girl from back in the day," Kayne said, all the while not taking his eyes off of me.

"You ol' girl? Oh shit, nigga! Damn!" Chris was in shock himself. I wondered what all Kayne had told him, but at the moment it didn't even matter. "Here, nigga, take my key, my room is empty." Chris handed Kayne his room key.

"Thanks. My bad, no hard feelings?"

"It's cool, man," Kayne reassured.

I reached out to give Chris a friendly hug. "I'ma still get some of that," he whispered into my ear as we embraced. He broke our embrace then looked at Kayne. "You still makin' them runs with me, right?"

"You know it." They dapped, then Chris retreated back into the smoke-filled room. When Kayne and I got to Chris' room, directly across the hall, I grabbed Kayne's hand and led him to the king-sized bed. I wanted to tell him what Chris said, but it wasn't the right time. I couldn't believe I was with Kayne again, and I wasn't about to fuck it up. I pushed him down gently, and straddled his lap with my clothes still on. I began kissing his neck the way I used to when he would get mad at me. He let me while he ran both his hands up my shirt and unsnapped my bra.

"Wait." I attempted to push him away from me. Guilt was weighing heavily on my mind. "This was a really bad way for us to meet up again, and I just want you to—"

"Shhh ..." he whispered, putting his finger to my lips.

I licked his finger, then slowly sucked it the way I used to. He replaced his finger with his lips, reclaiming what was his. "I missed you," Kayne whispered between kisses. He pulled my bra off and cupped both of my breasts, suck-

ing on them one at a time. Just that little bit took me over the top; I was ready to feel him inside of me. Taking his time, he stood up with my legs wrapped around him and laid me on my back. He pulled my shorts off, finding that I didn't have panties on.

"You was gonna give all this away to somebody else?" he asked, admiring my body. I knew he was jealous because of the look that only he could give.

"I'm sorry, daddy. It's yours now," I said, going for his jeans. He stopped me and knelt down, pulling me toward his face, licking and sucking up all the juices he and Chris had already produced. After two minutes, I was literally grinding on his face. It felt so good, I couldn't control myself. The wilder I got, the deeper he went. His tongue went in and out, making me anxious for his dick to make the same motion.

"Kayne, I need you to fuck me," I moaned, finishing my third orgasm. He stood up and slowly undressed, revealing my favorite thing in the whole world. His dick sprang free in anticipation of new, but familiar, territory. We held constant eye contact until I licked my lips and teased the head with my tongue. I then took his length, deep throating him. "Ummm ..." I hummed, bathing him in warm saliva. It had to be the best head I had ever given in my life, and it probably felt better for me than him. I put my whole heart into sucking his dick, and didn't even flinch when I felt the thickness of his cum trickle down my throat. I swallowed it like it was Kool-Aid then lay back and spread my legs, ready for the main course. As vulgar as our foreplay was, the act was love making in the strongest sense. I had never felt as much passion in my life. When he finally entered me, tears streamed down my face. He wiped each one away then kissed me lightly on my lips.

"I love you, Amina. I don't ever want to bring you no more tears. I'm gon' make you happy, I promise," he whispered. I couldn't help but cry even harder, until the pleasure of him inside my stomach made me stop and concentrate on throwing it back. We continued, non-stop, until the next morning.

We lay exhausted, intertwined, full of sweat, with more questions than answers. With a kiss he got up to turn on a hot shower. He didn't have to ask me to join him because I knew that was his intention. In the shower, he washed me from head to toe, and I enjoyed the feel of his body through the slippery soap as I caressed him. When we were both out, we sat on the bed in white towels, overwhelmed. I decided to speak first.

"So now what?" I asked, still debating if I was going to let him in on all the information I knew.

"Now, let's go home." He leaned over to kiss me.

"Where is home for you, Kayne? Tell me that," I spat angrily, dodging his kiss. He looked confused and shocked by my tone. Before he could answer, we were interrupted by the loud vibration of his cell phone on the nightstand. I watched him hesitate to answer. He finally did in an agitated tone.

"Yeah," he answered. My female intuition told me it was Marla. I never took my eyes off of him. "I'll be there." He hung up.

"Gotta go already?" I remarked, rolling my eyes.

"Mina, cut the bullshit, you know it ain't like that. I'll explain everything in the car. Get dressed. I'm taking you home."

"No, thanks. I'll call a cab, but it's been real." I got up to find my clothes, which were scattered all around the room. Kayne walked up behind me, grabbing me by the hips. Kissing the back of my neck, he whispered, "I love you, you know that. Nothing's changed. Let me take you home, baby. I promise I'll be there after I handle this. I'm coming home to you, and I ain't leaving no more." A part of me wanted to go buck wild on him and tell him everything I knew, but his touch melted me like candle wax. I was literally weak. I decided to wait and see exactly how long it would take him to tell me what I already knew.

Saying nothing, I continued to get dressed. I went to the lobby to wait on him while he found Chris to return his key. When we were finally in the car I noticed the envelope I sent to him on the passenger's seat floor. He picked it up, made sure it was sealed and shoved it into the glove compartment.

"Where we headed?" he asked.

"The EdgeCliff Condos," I told him with attitude.

"I know where that's at."

"Good, 'cause I ain't no fucking MapQuest." When we got to my condo, I was expecting him to drop me off at the front door. Instead he parked.

"What are you doing? I don't need you to walk me up if that's what you're thinking." I opened the door to get out, and so did he. He hit the car alarm as he followed me inside. "I thought you had more important things to do."

"Fuck what I had to do. Ain't shit more important than you, I mean that." I didn't respond as I entered the elevator to reach my floor.

"When you get this spot?" Kayne questioned as soon as I opened the door to my spacious home.

"I just got home in July. Zelle got me this."

"This is real nice," he said, admiring the surroundings. "You doing your thing as usual, huh?"

"You know it, baby." I threw my purse onto the couch and went to my bedroom where I locked the door behind me. I had been doing a good job of playing cool, but in reality, Kayne's presence brought on so many different emotions that I was completely overwhelmed. Our reunion was beautiful and even better than I had dreamed of, but I couldn't help but wonder where all of this would lead.

After gaining control of myself, I changed clothes and looked at the Caller ID. Two calls from Kelly, one from my mom and another from Good Samaritan Hospital. I made Kayne wait alone in the living room while I returned calls. Kelly and my mom were just checking in with me. Lastly, I called Marla's cell to be ahead of the game. I had to know if she called Kayne earlier.

"Hey girl, what's up?" I said cheerfully.

"Hey, who is this?" She sounded exhausted.

"It's me, girl, Mya. Did you have the baby? I saw a hospital number on my Caller ID."

"Yeah, this morning at five fifteen."

"So, he came early, huh? I bet you're happy about that.

How much did he weigh, what's his name?" I asked, faking excitement.

"He was seven pounds, six ounces. I named him Isaiah Timothy. Timothy was my grandfather's name."

"Well congratulations, sweetie. I'll be by to visit probably tomorrow. You sound really tired, and I don't want to keep you up."

"Yeah girl, they got me all drugged up, but stop by when you can." She yawned in my ear and continued, "I could use the company."

"Nobody's there with you?" I sounded concerned.

"Not right now. My sister had to go to work, and my mom is on her way back from out of town."

"Girl, where is Keon?"

"We'll talk."

"Okay, well get your rest. I get off at three tomorrow."

"Okay, I'll see you then."

When I walked back into the living room, Kayne was lounging on my couch with a Coke in his hand.

"I see you had no problem making yourself at home," I said, still playing the attitude role. Truthfully, seeing him comfortable in my home formed butterflies in my stomach.

"I see you had no problem making yourself at home either. You went and slipped into something a little more comfortable," he said, referring to my wife beater and boy shorts.

"Boy, quit," I giggled as he reached out and pulled me by my hands onto his lap.

"Why you have me sitting out here by myself for so

long? Had to go call your man and make sure he wasn't on his way home?"

"So, what were you going to explain to me in the car?" I asked, ignoring his comment.

"Just that I love you, and I missed you, and I'm sorry for everything you went through." Although his lips spoke the words, his eyes were telling the truth.

"That's it? You're sorry for everything I went through?" I spoke with an attitude. I was really enjoying giving him a hard time.

"What else you wanna hear, baby?" Kayne rubbed my back affectionately.

"The truth."

"That is the truth."

"Okay, why didn't we go to your house? I wanna see what you living like."

"Not as large as you." He looked around my condo and continued, "A nigga fresh out." His hands moved from my back to my thighs, but even that couldn't throw me off.

"So, what you living like then?"

"Nothing extravagant. Staying between Chris and my other nigga house right now." He didn't even flinch as he lied to me.

"And where is that?"

"Chris' spot is in Forest Park, and my other nigga got a spot in Westwood." At least he didn't say Fairfield. I stared into his eyes silently until I felt tears forming in my own. He had no intention of telling me about Marla. Still, I decided to wait it out. I had to know if he was worth all the pain he had caused.

"So, you staying or what?" I got up off of his lap. "I'm gonna take a nap." I went into my bedroom, knowing he would follow behind. He knew I couldn't resist him, but I knew he couldn't resist me either. One thing he didn't know was that he didn't have to worry about hurting me anymore because I was already hurt. As he held me and slept, I stayed awake crying as quietly as I could, finally dozing off to sleep.

A few hours later, I woke up from my nap to an empty bed. I was convinced that Kayne had left until I heard his phone vibrate on the nightstand. I picked it up and the Caller ID displayed Marla's name and her cell phone number. It continued to vibrate. I put it down just in case Kayne returned. A minute later a text came through:

> The least you can do is pick up the phone. I know you're upset but Isaiah is yours. Come see him for yourself. If you want a test I will give you one. Please don't make me go through this alone.

I erased the message because it was already opened. I heard Kayne walking toward the door and I quickly put the phone down, burying myself under the sheets, pretending to be asleep. He lightly shook me. I opened my eyes to a tray of delicious breakfast—five perfect pancakes, smothered in syrup, an omelet with green peppers and onions and six slices of turkey bacon. Breakfast was the only meal he ever cooked, and it was always delicious.

"Baby, you didn't have to do all this." I sat up as he put the tray in front of me.

"I know, but I wanted to fix you something." He smiled

proudly. I found it adorable that he took the time to cook for me.

"I didn't even realize I had all this in my kitchen. Come here, baby." I pulled the covers back. "I can't eat all this by myself. You have to help me." He got back in the bed with me and we took turns feeding each other. After eating we went for round two of our room-shaking sex. The sound of his phone vibrating the whole time only made each stroke better.

Chapter 12

Monday—August 28, 2006

I got up feeling very refreshed. Kayne and I did a whole lot of talking, but he still hadn't broken the news yet. He wanted to focus on now, and let the past go. I told myself that he was afraid to tell me the truth, or maybe he wanted to get a paternity test before he spilled the beans for no reason. Either way, I was growing impatient with him. He was still asleep when I got up for work, so I was surprised to see him brushing his teeth at the sink when I stepped out of the shower.

"Hey, baby, did the shower wake you up?" I asked, dropping my towel, ready to get fixed real good before I left for work.

"Probably. You want me to drive you to work and pick you up?" I had told him I worked at a different nursing

home on the opposite side of town from my real job. Even though he hadn't been honest with me yet, I felt like shit for lying to him.

"No, but I want you to make me cum before I leave," I told him with a hand on my hip, looking impatient. He gave me a grin as he put the toothbrush up and followed me to the bedroom where he gave me the most amazing head ever given.

"You be good while mommy is gone. I'll be home by five," I said, kissing him on the lips as he lay in the bed, flipping through channels. I wanted to stay so bad.

"I ain't leaving. I'll be right here when you get home. So don't be long." He smacked me on the ass before I turned to leave. God, I wished I could stay. I knew I didn't necessarily need my job, but it was an obligation.

After getting off of work at three, I went straight over to the hospital to see Marla. I called to check on Kayne on my way. As he said he would be, he was still at home waiting on me. I told him I was stopping to visit Gary, who I'd told him about the night before. In the gift shop at the hospital I purchased a balloon, a teddy bear and a card for Marla. I quickly found her room after asking at the front desk.

"Knock, knock," I called out as I entered the room.

"Hey, girl." She sounded excited to see me. "I'm just laying him back down. He just fell asleep." She gently laid the baby in the small container-looking crib that all hospitals provide.

"Awww, I missed him," I said, setting the bear and balloon down on the window sill with the other two teddy bears and cards she had. I handed her my card.

"Thanks, girl, you didn't have to bring anything. You're so sweet." She smiled, opening the card. She read it aloud, and thanked me again with a hug. I sat down in the chair across from her bed.

"I want to hold little man. Let me wash my hands." As I held her son, all kinds of things ran through my head, from the baby I had lost to the fact that this could be Kayne's child, birthed by another woman. I was almost grateful that he slept as I held him. I don't think I could have handled looking into his eyes.

"Who does the baby look like?"

"Well, I think he's got my head, but his features remind me of Keon's, though it could just be wishful thinking. My older sister thinks he looks like Jason, only because she's never seen Keon. She stays so busy she probably won't meet him until the wedding. She's not too thrilled about me marrying a man with no career anyway."

"What does your mother think?" I asked suddenly, feeling the need to pry.

"She met him once and really didn't have much to say. My mother's just like that. Her whole motto is whatever floats your boat."

"He smells so good." I sniffed. "I love the smell of a new baby." I smiled. "How are things with you and Keon now? I know he's a proud daddy."

"Yeah, he spent the night with us last night. He left early this morning to go home and clean up for the baby. I go home tomorrow." She lied without even blinking.

"What's up with Jason? How's he taking things?"

"He's been dying to come see the baby, but I just can't

risk him bumping heads with Keon."

"Don't risk it then, make him wait. You are getting a test, right?"

"Yeah, when I get the nerve to tell Kayne that we need a test," she lied again.

"It'll work out, just take your time and don't stress."

"Yeah, I will."

I got up to lay the baby back down. "Sorry I have to leave so soon. I have to pick my mom up from work. Call me when you get home and get settled okay?" I told her as I gave her a hug.

"I will. Thanks for stopping by."

"Okay, take care of that precious baby, I'll be checking on you."

"Okay." I walked out feeling like the champion of a fight Marla didn't even know she was fighting. Call me a home wrecker if you want, but I had to be the best of my kind.

In the elevator I saw Nurse Davis. She had cared for me when I lost my baby three years earlier after some chicks jumped me in Saks and stabbed me in the stomach. It wasn't Kayne's baby. I had gotten pregnant by some dead beat named Maurice before Kayne and I met.

"Hi, how have you been doing?" She smiled, excited to see me.

"Great, how are you?"

"Doing good, just working hard. You look really good!"

"Thanks, you too. It was nice seeing you," I said as I exited the elevator. I rushed to my car, anxious to get away from the hospital before my mind started drifting to thoughts of having a baby.

* * * *

When I walked in the door I could hear Kayne all the way from my bedroom yelling at someone on the phone.

"Didn't I say I would be there? Don't keep calling me. I'm coming, damn!" He paused for a minute. "And it don't matter where I'm at, I'll be there when I get there!"

I pretended not to notice his conversation as I walked into the room while he clipped his cell back on his hip. As Kayne spoke, his whole expression changed. I walked up to him, sliding my arms around his waist.

"I talked to your mama. She called about ten minutes ago." He looked and smelled so fresh I wanted to keep him from going to see her.

"Oh, really? What did you two talk about?" The look on his face was one of relief. He just knew I was going to ask about what I had just heard.

"She knew who I was when I told her my name. She just said she wants us to come over to Gary's next Sunday so she can meet me."

"You bullshitting me, right?"

"No, why would I lie about that? I never met her. Don't you think it's about time, or ain't we on the same terms as back in the day?" He gave me a serious look while waiting for a response.

"We on better terms than ever," I said, kissing him softly on the lips. "Where you think you going anyway?" I asked as he squeezed my ass, pulling me closer.

"Make some runs."

"So you leaving me here by myself?"

"Just for a little while." He gave me a kiss then grabbed his keys. I didn't follow him to the door like Marla would have, but as soon as the thought of him holding her baby ran through my mind, I immediately became furious. Anger seemed to be rising up rapidly inside of me. I couldn't stand to see him run to her side when I wanted him here with me.

"Kayne, we need to talk," I spat angrily, just as he was getting ready to leave.

"Baby, can it wait till I get back? I won't be gone long."

"No, it can't. I wanna talk now!" I was pissed for so many reasons.

He read my mood and sat down on the couch. "I'm listening, baby."

"No, I'm listening, and this time, you will be doing all the talking. I want some answers."

"Answers to what, Mina?" He looked confused.

"What happened the day you got locked up?"

"Damn, we gotta go back there?"

"Yep," I said, agitated.

He paused momentarily before speaking. "Well, two days before my spot got busted, somebody snitched on me and told the police I was staying at my cousin's where me and you was. I went outside to get something from the car that morning, and you know the rest." He was leaving Shalauna out.

"Who snitched?"

"This chick who ran the trap. It was her house, so she got charged with everything." Finally some honesty.

"Why didn't I know you was trapping out of some

bitch's house?"

"It didn't matter because every night I was coming home to you."

"Whatever!" I gave him the hand. "What did you get charged with?"

He looked at me closely, trying to figure out where I was going with my inquiries. "Conspiracy with intent to distribute."

"What?" I asked.

"They had to put some bullshit charge on me, but in reality, the only thing I had on me was some cash and weed. Remember, we smoked the night before."

"You're right," I recalled. "So why didn't your lawyer tell me this?"

"Because at the time we didn't know what was going on. They were trying to pin me with distribution, possession, money laundering—"

"Money laundering? How much did you have on you?"

"I didn't keep a lot on me when I realized we were being watched. I only had about twenty grand on me but that in itself was too much to explain. So, I ain't say shit. It wasn't until after you was already gone that I found out she snitched. Mina, you and I were both locked up on some bullshit. I couldn't see you, I couldn't even tell you what went down in a letter. Every day I sat in that cell and prayed that one day I'd be sitting in front of you like I am right now, telling you the truth." He sounded relieved.

"One day? Kayne, I was looking at twenty-one years for selling to an undercover officer. Were you going to wait for me that long?"

"Yes, if that's what it took. Mina, where is all this shit coming from?"

"It's coming from here, Kayne." I pointed toward my heart. "I gave up a lot for you and I deserve to know everything." He nodded in agreement. "Why did you let my peoples keep you from me while I was away?"

"Because I knew I had hurt you, and honestly, I didn't believe I deserved to see you at the time. I'm happy to have you back in my life now and hope that we can put the past behind us. I love you." He pulled me close and kissed my lips.

"Just leave." I backed up from him. "And don't come back."

"What?" He looked hurt.

"You heard me."

Kayne looked at me, turned around and said nothing as he walked out the door. I felt like I had made the biggest mistake of my life.

Chapter 13

Friday—September 8, 2006

It had been almost two weeks since I'd seen Kayne. He called three days in a row, but after that, I didn't hear from him again. I knew if he wasn't in the streets with Chris, he was at home with Marla and the baby, and as far as I was concerned, that was where he could stay. I told my mother he would be out of town for a while because of a death in the family so that she would finally stop bugging me about when they would meet.

I had done all kinds of things since Kayne had been gone to keep my mind clear, from going to movies alone to visiting the museum. Today, I decided shopping would be a good outlet. After spending more money than I planned, I was heading out of the mall with a handful of bags when someone grabbed me lightly by the arm.

"Where you headed?" It was Chris.

"Home." I couldn't help but smile. He was looking even better than the first time I saw him. This seemed like the perfect opportunity to get my mind off Kayne.

"Oh, for real. How you and my nigga doing?"

"Haven't spoken to him in a while," I said coolly, trying not to seem pressed.

"I saw the baby the other day. Lil' nigga look just like him to me." It was obvious he was trying to throw the shit up in my face, but he wouldn't see me sweat.

"Yeah well, I'm happy for him," I lied.

"It's cool that you ain't tripping about him marrying his baby mama and all. I know y'all probably had something a long time ago, but I'm trying to see what's up right now." He looked me dead in the eyes and I could tell he was serious. Kayne had really fucked my head and heart up, and revenge smelled so sweet. I gave him my number with a promise to hook up with him the next night.

As soon as I made it in the door with my bags, Marla was calling. I had only talked to her a handful of times since Kayne left. Normally, hearing the baby in the background only made me want to cut the conversation short, crawl in my bed and cry over spilled milk. Today, I felt up to talking.

"Hey, girl, where you at?" She sounded so cheerful.

"Just getting in from the mall. What's up?"

"Nothing, girl, I was just calling to see if you might want to stop by. Keon is out of town, and I need some company. I'll even cook!"

"No, girl, you don't need to be cooking. We can order

in, or I can pick up something."

"Well, pizza sounds good to me. We'll order when you get here." After she gave me directions, which I already knew, I called Zelle to see if he knew if Kayne was out of town. Zelle and Kelly were in Jamaica, and I hated to disturb them, but I had to be safe. I was actually surprised that Zelle knew Kayne's whereabouts. They were obviously becoming close again. He told me Kayne left the night before on a trip to Detroit. Zelle had given him a new connect.

The front door of Marla's townhouse was unlocked when I arrived. She was on the couch breast feeding her son. Their home looked so comfortable—a huge leather sectional, plasma TV and pictures of her and her family adorned the living room walls. I looked around for photos of Marla and Kayne. There was one on the table beside the couch.

"This must be Keon?" I scoped every detail of the framed picture. They were hugged up on the couch together. Marla looked happy holding his hands on her pregnant belly while Kayne looked distant.

"Yeah, that's my baby." She smiled proudly. "That's not a really good picture, but it's the only one I have of us. I can't wait to take our wedding pictures."

"Men always try to look hard," I commented, posing like a nigga in the club.

"Ain't that right?" Marla agreed. "But he better smile in these wedding pictures like his shoes are too tight," Marla joked, grimacing. We both laughed.

"Hey, can I use your bathroom?"

"Yeah, straight up the steps and to the right," she told me, shifting the baby who was having a hard time latching onto her nipple. "The toilet down here is messed up. They're coming to fix it Monday."

I walked upstairs to the restroom, which sat between Marla's room and the baby's room. I noticed two toothbrushes sitting out—a sign that he still lived there. I also saw tons of his shoes lined across her bedroom floor, and call me crazy but I swore I could smell his scent coming from her room. Curiosity lured me inside. I opened the nightstand drawer to find an open box of condoms and a tube of KY Jelly. There was also a picture of Marla and some dark-skinned, hood-rat-looking chick with a fucked up weave. On the back it read, "Me and Shalauna – Summer 2005." I also found a piece of paper folded up. I opened it and read it. It was an email from Jason dated three days ago.

Marla, I want you to know I still love you and always will. But you also need to know that since we saw your friend at dinner and I was mistaken for Keon, I've been feeling really played. I need to know where your heart really is, because last night you seemed so distant. It felt like I was there alone. I don't want to be your Plan B. If you don't break up with him soon, I want nothing to do with you or Isaiah. I can't let you continue to hurt me. I hope you understand this. I love you, please know that.

Jason.

I folded the paper up and put it back into the drawer.

"Do you like Donatos?" Marla yelled up the steps just as I was on my way down.

"Yeah that sounds good. What kind of pizza?"

"I like The Works. Everything's on it."

"That's fine. Order some wings, too," I said, picking Isaiah up. I played with him, making funny noises and faces that made him smile, while Marla ordered our food. He had the same light complexion as Marla, but had beady eyes that reminded me of Jason's. I looked closely at him trying to find anything that resembled Kayne. I didn't find anything.

Marla put Isaiah to sleep before the pizza was delivered so that we could eat in peace.

"So, girl, tell me a little more about what you did before you came to work at Blue Sky."

I prepared to use my imagination. This would be fun.

"Okay. You might not believe me though."

"Try me."

"I was living in Detroit with my boyfriend, Tre'mar. You know, the one I told you was locked up?" She nodded. "Well, Tre'mar was a nigga with a good game. He could talk a bitch into doing damn near anything. So when he asked me to sell my body for money so that we could be rich, I agreed. And that's what I did for about a year. I turned tricks every night bringing in big money, at least a thousand a night. Then Tre'mar caught an assault charge for beating some bitch who tried to steal from him. He was trying to make an example out of her so that none of his other hoes would be dumb enough to try anything so stupid.

"Well anyway, to make a long story short, he went to jail and I came here where my mother is and started working with her at a cleaning service. I worked there for about a month until I met this white girl named Kara on the internet who owned an escort service. It was nothing like being out on the streets. I was basically going on dates with high profile white men to different events. I mostly did local dates, but sometimes I was sent out of town with men to different places." By now Marla's mouth was on the floor. I could tell she was judging me by the look in her eyes. Not necessarily like I was a slut, but more like she was jealous that I was caking up. It was time for me to turn it up a notch.

"Those were the best dates. I loved traveling to places like Vegas and Miami. Most of the men were respectable, but that's not to say that I didn't come across a few perverts, because believe me, white men can be some nasty fucks sometimes. But overall, I enjoyed working for the service. I quit a month before I came to Blue Sky because Tre'mar told me he didn't want me selling myself anymore. He told me he regretted ever putting the woman he loved out on the track like he did. He says when he gets home he wants to get married and move away.

"So I'm just waiting for my baby to be free so that I can live the life I've always wanted, you know? After a while a ho just gets tired of the fast lane. It just wasn't for me anymore. I became very wealthy in the process, but at the same time, I lost a lot of myself. I'm enjoying working at Blue Sky, earning my money the honest way." I wished I could capture the look on Marla's face.

"Wow, girl, that's some story," she said, still unable to believe it.

"Yeah, and you're the only one I've ever told. So I hope this stays between me and you because people are so quick to turn their noses up and judge."

"Of course, girl. And you know I'm not here to judge you. I wish you and Tre'mar luck with the engagement, too. That's great."

"Thanks." The pizza man rang the doorbell.

"So do you have any idea where you want your wedding?" she asked, handing me a plate.

"Nope, I told myself I wouldn't think about any of that until Tre'mar is out and we can make plans together." I grabbed a few wings and two slices of pizza.

"Yeah, I can understand that. It's better if you do it together. It makes it so exciting," she said.

"Speaking of that," I said, biting into my pizza, "how are your wedding plans going?"

"Pretty good. Keon wants to do the outside wedding thing, so we'll probably be looking at June. He's picked his boy Chris to be his Best Man. Speaking of Chris, what's up with the one you met?"

"Girl, nothing at all. We're just friends. Like I told you, I met him at the club a few weeks ago, and we just went out for drinks that one time. I actually haven't talked to him since."

"Oh, okay."

"Sounds like everything with you and Keon is good. He's enjoying doing the wedding plans with you?"

"Girl, yes, I'm so happy. For a minute, I thought we

were falling apart. I can't wait for my stomach to go down so I can go get fitted for my dress. Keon already picked out his tux. Our colors are going to be white and pale yellow." She was lying, and I knew it. Sitting in her house, I felt sort of guilty, but in a good way. In a matter of weeks I was going to rip this household apart. First on my to do list: hurt Kayne in the worst way.

Chapter 14

Saturday—September 9, 2006

Chris picked me up at nine o'clock. We went across the river for drinks at Tropicana. After our first drink, Chris told me how he'd met Kayne during his four-year bid. The two became cool, and Kayne used to talk about me often, but he never told Chris why I was locked up. I told him the whole story of what happened and how I caught a felony trying to keep Kayne from the four years that he ended up doing two and a half of anyway. Chris was shocked to say the least, but he seemed to gain a little more respect for me.

Chris told me about his first love, his baby mama, who he had since gotten a restraining order against because she was insanely jealous, and for good reason—Chris was fine, and he knew it. Four drinks later, I got wet thinking about

what he could do. It would only be a one night stand, I reasoned. Fuck it! I excused myself to go to the restroom. Moments later, I walked back to our booth and saw Chris talking to a female while he paid for the bill. Once I got closer, I almost pissed my pants. It was Marla! For a split second I thought about sneaking out and catching a cab home, but with Marla knowing me as someone else, I was sure I would have no problem.

"Hey, girl," I greeted her with a surprised look.

"Chris, is this your girl? It's such a small world! We work together." Marla smiled.

"We're just friends," he told her, "but yeah, I guess it is a small world."

"Chris is actually really good friends with Keon," Marla informed me while patting him on the back. "He's the one I told you about who will be the Best Man at our wedding." I had to get away before one of them tried to mention my name.

"Oh really? Girl, look at you trying to look all good after having that baby," I laughed, trying to change the subject.

"Girl, you know I had to get out the house. I'm waiting on my sister. She's running late." She looked at her watch. "But I'll let you two go. Enjoy the rest of your night." She winked at me.

"I plan on it." I winked back at her. "Call me."

She smiled at us both as we headed out. I was so relieved not to be busted.

"That was weird as hell," Chris said as we walked to his car.

"Yeah, she doesn't know I know Kayne, and he doesn't

know that I know her, but that's between me and you," I confided, sliding into the front seat of his Impala. He closed the door and walked to the other side.

Now in the driver's seat, Chris leaned over with one thing in mind. "Right, I know some other things I want to keep between us, too." He moved one side of my low-cut halter top to the side and licked my nipple. I could tell he was all about getting some pussy and that was it. I didn't even care if he kept anything about that night between us. I planned on throwing it up in Kayne's face anyway.

"Oooh, baby, you moving fast ain't you?" I lifted his head up.

"I'm sorry. I just been wanting to get a taste of you since that night at the club. You gon' let me do that?" He looked at me, licking his lips slowly.

"Of course." I climbed into the back seat and pulled my jeans and panties completely off. He followed behind me and dove into my pussy, face first. I was shocked but satisfied. Chris licked and slurped up every last drop of my wetness like he was competing for a trophy. He made me cum twice. When I couldn't take any more I pushed his head away, letting him know I was ready for penetration. He pulled out his dick and inserted it so quickly that I never even got a glance to see what he was working with. As he slid inside of me, I wondered why he didn't put on a condom, but before I could question it, he was going to work. He was diving in deeper with each stroke, and I was convinced he was trying to drill another hole. His dick was so big and hard that I winced from the pain, but never one to be scared of a dick, I bit my lip and turned the pain into

pleasure by grinding my hips onto him hard and throwing my pussy right back at him. Within five minutes I was cumming. A few minutes later he followed my lead, pulling out and nutting all over my leg.

"That was some good-ass pussy," he said, attempting to put himself back in me.

"Uh uh," I told him. "Can't be greedy," I teased, but I was really tripping off the fact that he hadn't worn a condom.

Smirking, he reached up under his seat and pulled out an old shirt. He wiped my leg off, then wiped his dick and pulled his pants back up. He felt around and found my panties and jeans then handed them to me.

"You good, shorty?" Chris asked once we climbed back into the front seat and got situated.

"Yeah, I'm straight. I'm just tired."

He grinned like he just really put the shit on me. He did, but I wasn't about to let him know it. I just wanted to get back home and be alone. Chris checked his voicemail and made calls, which meant he didn't have to talk to me. I didn't mind though because it gave me the much needed time to think and pray that there wouldn't be any repercussions from the bad choice I had just made. I looked at Chris as he drove and the truth was in my face—he was a nasty snake, and even with me knowing this I let myself get bitten.

We pulled into my parking lot. Before I got out, I looked at him. "Thanks, I had a good time," I said, giving him a fake smile.

"Me too, baby. I'll call you so we can do this again sometime."

With the same fake smile, I got out of his car, hoping I would never see him again.

Good sex, no matter how wrong it was, followed by a hot shower, always resulted in a great sleep for me. But mine was disturbed by a loud knock at door at three fifteen in the morning.

"Hold on, I'm coming, damn!" I yelled, throwing on a robe. Whoever was knocking sounded like they were trying to beat the door down. Looking through the peep hole I saw Kayne standing there with an angry look on his face.

"What the fuck is your problem knocking on my door at this hour?" I spat angrily as he brushed past me and went into my room.

"You just now getting home?" he asked, looking at me like I was dirt on the bottom of his shoe.

"No, does it look like I just got home? Nigga, I was asleep!"

"I just figured you and Chris had a late night, that's all, *Mya*." I was completely tongue tied. "When was you going to let me know you was best friends with my baby mama and that you was fucking my boy!" I had never seen him so pissed in my life.

"After you told me that you had a baby mama!"

"I was going to tell you."

"When Kayne? I gave you every opportunity!"

"After I figured some shit out."

"After you figured out what? How you could be with both of us at the same time?"

"No, it ain't shit like that, Mina. I don't even know if the baby is mine. She's fucking somebody else."

"You think I don't know that?"

"What you mean by that?"

"I was the one who sent the pictures."

"What! What the fuck type shit you on?"

"I'm on getting you back, destroying the bitch who tried to steal you and hurting you all at the same time!" Tears fell from my eyes without permission.

"Come here, baby." He grabbed me and pulled me into his arms. "You don't have to do this. We was going to be together regardless. I told you a long time ago we would be together again. I was never going to marry her, I was just waiting on the right time to let her go. But now that I know she's a scandalous bitch, it's only going to make it easier."

"She told you she saw me?"

"Yeah, she came home talking—"

"Home?" I spat. Hearing him call another woman's place home didn't sit well with me. "I'm staying between Chris and my other nigga house," I mimicked. "She yo' nigga now?"

Shocked at my reaction and remembering what he said, Kayne continued, "When she got back to the house, she started talking about how Chris was out with her best friend from work. It wasn't the first time she mentioned Mya, but it was the first time I paid attention. She described you a little, saying you really was Chris' type, then it hit me. I called Chris a little later to see what he was up to, and he was fumbling for words, real shook. I knew that night I saw you at the hotel and he fell back after realizing you was my chick that the nigga still wanted to fuck

with you. Nigga ain't shit."

"Well, the truth is out, so now what?" I dried my eyes, feeling a little bad for what I'd done.

"Now, I'm going to find out if the baby is mine."

"And if it is?"

"Then I'll take care of my son, but regardless, you and me, we gonna be together. In the meantime, don't fuck with anyone else. I couldn't really demand that of you before because I was with Marla, but that shit is a wrap. You my girl now, and if I hear of another nigga touching you, you will be coming to visit me in prison 'cause I'm killing him." He walked out of the room. I felt so low.

"Where are you going?" I followed him to the door.

"I gotta get out of here, Mina."

"Wait, I'm sorry," I said, forcing him to hold me.

"What do you wanna do? I can't be with you if you keep trying to get payback."

"I know, baby, and the only people I want to get back are Marla for stealing you from me and her cousin for snitching on you and separating us for so long."

"Me too, baby."

I didn't expect those words to come out of Kayne's mouth. All of a sudden, I became angry. He wasn't on this shit before I mentioned it.

"Why, Kayne?"

"Why what?"

"Why would you possibly want to set Marla up? You do have a baby by her," I said sarcastically.

"Like I said, I don't know if the baby is mine, and shit ... fuck Marla, she was something to do until my baby

came back." He kissed me on my forehead. "Now her cousin on the other hand ..."

"What about her? What you gonna get out of it?"

"It's simple," he said calmly.

"Well, simplify my life and tell me!" I yelled.

"She cop from Derrick."

"Derrick? The one who set me up?"

"Yep."

I didn't know what to say.

"We ended up bumping heads through Chris. That's one of his boys."

I shook my head in disgust. "You know what, Kayne, it doesn't surprise me. All dirty snakes run together."

Kayne didn't comment on my remark. Instead, he continued speaking. "They go way back. Since he left the city, he been living in Kentucky as a supplier. The nigga got pretty good product and always hook me up for the low. Anyway, the nigga owe me, Mina. Besides the money, he gotta pay for what he did to you. He had the nerve to lie and tell me he didn't know the drop that day was a set up. I let him believe shit was cool, but I ain't no damn fool. Now Chris ... the nigga know you my girl, and he still didn't give a fuck. With him ..." Kayne went into deep thought, then smiled at me. "Baby, we gonna do this?"

"Let's do it."

We were finally on the same page.

Chapter 15

Sunday—September 10, 2006

Kayne had me call my mother to schedule dinner for the evening, his treat. I was so excited that they were finally going to meet. On our way out to my car, I couldn't help but wonder what my mother would think of Kayne. When I saw my car, I stopped in my tracks. My good mood was ruined. My front windshield was completely shattered, my paint was keyed, "home wrecker" was spray painted on the driver's side, and on the passenger's side the word "bitch" stared back at me in red paint. I think I felt steam coming out of my ears. I ran over to the driver's side to see if anything was taken but before I could open the door, Kayne stopped me.

"Step back. Let me look inside first."

I was so pissed I couldn't even speak. Suddenly my

phone rang.

"Hello!" I answered angrily.

"Amina, it's Chris. I'm calling to let you know my baby mama followed us to your crib last night, and she told me she fucked your car up."

"I see that, nigga! How in the fuck did she even know where my car was if I rode with you?"

"She told me she saw you get out of my car and get something out of your truck. I'm sorry, and I'll pay for all of the damages."

"You got that right, nigga!" I yelled into the phone.

"One of my niggas got a shop and—"

"I don't give a damn who got a shop, Chris. What I do know is, you better get it first thing in the morning and get my shit fixed … and don't let me catch yo' baby mama!" I yelled into the phone, then ended the call.

I remembered going to my car last night to get my cell phone charger.

"You know your doors was unlocked and the alarm wasn't set?" Kayne told me as he finished inspecting the inside.

"No shit!" I said angrily, walking back inside and dialing my mother as I rode the elevator back to my apartment, leaving Kayne outside.

"Hey, Ma, we're going to have to cancel dinner. My car was vandalized last night."

"Vandalized by who?"

"I went out with this guy last night, and his baby mama followed us and messed my car up."

"You need to press charges on that crazy bitch, Amina."

"I know, Ma, I'll call you tomorrow. I need to just lay

down."

"Okay, baby. Is Kayne there with you?"

"Yeah, we're going to take care of everything, don't worry."

"Alright, I love you, and you be careful."

"Love you, too. I'll talk to you later."

Kayne walked in while I was sitting on the bed with my face in my hands. I couldn't believe this had happened to me.

"Was it worth it?"

"What?"

"Was fucking that nigga worth getting your car trashed?" I stood up and smacked him as hard as my strength would let me. Instead of hitting me back, he walked out of the room and answered his ringing cell phone.

"I'm on my way now," he said, then hung up immediately.

"Is that her? You on your way home to your snake-ass bitch?" I was ready to punch him now.

"I won't stay here and fight with you," Kayne told me, looking at me with hurt in his eyes.

"Just go!" I pushed him toward the front door. Kayne didn't budge, so I turned to go back to my room.

He grabbed me from behind. "I love you, baby. Can we start over?" Kayne spoke in a whisper and planted a soft kiss on my neck.

"It's too late. Everything is fucked up." I pulled away with no luck; he wasn't letting me go.

"It ain't too late. If I want you, and you want me, what's

the problem?"

"She's the problem, Kayne! You just told her you was on your way, stop playing games!"

"I know, on my way to go get my shit out of her house. I'll be back." He kissed me and left out before I could say anything more. I needed to talk to someone, so I called Kelly.

"Hey, girl, I got good news and bad news. Which one do you want first?" I asked her, not asking if she was tied up with anything at the minute.

"Bad."

"I went out with Chris last night to get back at Kayne. His baby mama followed us back here and fucked up my car." I left out the part about us boning in the back of his car.

"Fucked it up how?"

"She busted my front windshield and sprayed 'bitch' and 'home wrecker' on the doors. Even though Chris is gonna pay for it, if I catch the bitch, she dead!"

"Damn right! We'll find out who the salty bitch is. Now, give me the good news."

"Kayne and I are back together."

"What?!"

"Yeah, girl. He told me about everything that happened that night."

"Everything?" Kelly asked.

"Yeah, everything. You know he left out some names, but I was one up on his ass anyway."

Kelly laughed. "I'm so happy for you two!"

"Thanks, but hey, what's up with Butter? I need to know

where Shalauna is. Kayne knows what I wanna do, and now he wants in."

"Are you serious?"

"Yep."

"Alright then, I'll pick you up in an hour, and we can go holla at her. I know where to find her."

"Cool, I'll be ready."

Kayne came in twenty minutes later carrying three huge garbage bags full of clothes and shoes.

"Where you going?" he asked. I was changing into jeans and a shirt.

"Kelly's on her way to get me. We gotta go handle something. I won't be gone long." I headed to the kitchen for some ice water. When I walked back into the room, I noticed Kayne putting my cell phone back on the charger.

"What are you doing?"

"I told Kelly not to come. If we doing this, we gotta do it together."

"Yeah, but—"

"But, don't make no moves without me, and I won't make no moves without you. I knew you was up to something. I thought it was about the chick who fucked up the car, but you trying to get information and scheme without me." He sounded upset.

"Calm down. It ain't even like that, daddy. I was going to let you in as soon as I found out where Shalauna was." I smiled and Kayne looked shocked.

"How you know her name?"

I grabbed my jacket and walked out the door, with Kayne right behind me.

I never answered his question, but in the car I explained that Butter was the wife of the notorious Rome, who I knew he had heard of.

When we got to the Shell station downtown on Liberty, I spotted Butter right away. You could see her gold chain from a mile away. Her hair was still as long as ever and hanging down her back.

"Hey, lil' sis, it's been a long time! Get out that car and give me some love!" She embraced me. "How have you been?"

"Good, how you been?" I smiled, hugging her back.

"Girl, just trying to make it out here. You know how it is in these streets. Let's ride," she suggested, getting in the back seat of Kayne's Charger.

I introduced Butter to Kayne, who seemed honored to meet the wife of a city legend. Butter then let us in on everything about Shalauna that we needed to know, from the exact address of her new trap spot to who she was trapping with. Her spy let her know that Shalauna was, in fact, working closely with a new dope boy—none other than Kayne's cell block buddy, Chris.

Chapter 16

Tuesday—September 12, 2006

Chris did as he was told and got my car Monday morning. Surprisingly, Chris and Kayne continued business as usual with a promise to make another run soon. It disgusted me to see Kayne still cool with Chris, but that was part of the game—keep your enemies close. Kayne told me he'd drop me off and pick me up from work until I got my car back. With Marla out on maternity leave, we didn't have to worry about her seeing us. To lighten my mood, Kayne suggested that we have lunch with my mother today since I was off work. I agreed, and we met her at Pappadeaux at two o'clock.

"Ma, this is Keon. Keon, this is my mother, Kayla," I introduced them before we sat down.

"Hi, Keon, it's wonderful to finally meet you." My mother blushed as he shook her hand. Kayne had already told me that he wanted to be introduced to my mother using his real name out of respect.

"It's nice to meet you, too. I'm sorry it took so long." He pulled out both of our chairs.

"That's okay. I'm just happy everything is okay with Amina. She could have been hurt."

"You don't have to worry about that. Everything has been taken care of."

"Good." She looked at me. "Amina, I have great news."

"What?"

"The police found Markus last night. He's in custody now, and my lawyer says he's probably going to being charged with attempted murder."

"I'm glad they caught that bastard! Where did they find him?"

"He was staying in some motel in Hamilton. The owner saw his picture on the news and called Crime Stoppers."

"That's wonderful, Ma. I feel much better knowing he's behind bars and you're safe."

"How's Gary doing?" Kayne asked.

"He's actually doing great. He's getting around a lot better now, but he still has a little more healing to do."

"I'm glad to hear that," Kayne told her.

"Thanks, that's sweet of you to ask. How's your family doing? I know you just recently suffered a loss. I just want to offer my condolences." Luckily, I had already let Kayne know my mother would probably mention this.

"Everybody's doing good." Kayne looked at me, trying to remember the lie I'd told. "My aunt died of old age, you

know, but she lived a long happy life."

"How old was she?"

"Ninety."

"Wow, that's really a blessing to live that long."

"Yeah, it is." The waitress came and we all ordered. Kayne asked for a bottle of their best champagne to be brought out right away.

"I want to make a toast to you, Amina, the woman I love, and to you, Kayla, the woman who brought the best love I've ever had into this world. I love you both," Kayne said as we all touched glasses.

"Is he always this charming?" My mother giggled, eating him up.

"Yes, Mommy. He's always been the sweetest man I've known." I kissed Kayne on the lips.

"If my daughter's happy, then I'm happy. However, if something is wrong, I'll know it, remember that." She smiled, giving him a wink.

"I want nothing in the world but to make Amina happy. I know I made some mistakes in the past that hurt her, but I'm here now to make up for all of that, if you and she will let me."

"Baby, everybody in this world has made mistakes. As long as you both realize those mistakes are what make you stronger and smarter, you will find happiness together."

"It's funny you mentioned finding happiness together because that's exactly what I want to do." He got down on one knee, and I floated right up to cloud nine. "Amina, if I can't be happy with you, I can't be happy with anyone. You're all I want. Will you make me the happiest man alive by becoming my wife?" He held open a ring box that held a four carat diamond ring. My mother and I were both speechless. The ring he gave me wasn't nearly as big as Marla's, but the fact that he chose it and gave it to me was something more precious than she could ever know.

"Yes!" I finally managed to whisper as tears gathered in my eyes. I was overwhelmed with happiness. I had been dreaming of this day since the first time I'd laid eyes on Kayne. I kissed him as the whole restaurant began clapping. Kayne slid the beautiful ring onto my finger.

"Make my baby happy," my mother told him, giving him a huge hug.

"I plan on it." Kayne smiled proudly. He looked the happiest I had ever seen him.

"So, what are your plans for your life with Amina?" My mother asked as we all dug into our food.

"Well, I'm actually thinking about moving to Long Beach, where my mother is. My cousin sold me quite a bit of property out there. I plan on making some huge investments that will ensure Amina and our children security for the rest of their lives." I couldn't believe he already had plans for us. I was so proud of him.

"California? That's wonderful. How much property?"

"I purchased a small two-bedroom house that will have to be remodeled before I rent it out. I also have two two-bedroom condos. I'll rent one out, and Mina and I will stay in the other until we buy a house. How does that sound to you, baby?"

"I've never been to Cali, but I would love to go, baby. But if we are going to do this it's going to be you and me

together. I want to get in school so that I can have something to give our children, too."

"That's great, baby. What do want to study?"

"I guess business. I really want to open a bookstore." I let them both in on a dream I'd developed while incarcerated. "I love reading, and I've been wanting to own something of my own, after seeing Damen and Zelle do so well."

"Amina, that's wonderful! I had no idea that you wanted to open a bookstore, but if that's what you want, baby, you go for it! I am so proud of you. Although I really don't want to see you go, I think leaving Cincinnati would be a good thing for you. You need a brand new life, and I wish you two the best." My mother started getting teary-eyed.

"I'm proud of you, too, baby. We gon' make it happen for real. We a team now." Kayne smiled at me.

"Baby, you should have warned me this was going to be such an emotional day." I smiled, wiping tears from my own eyes again. The thought of starting over fresh in beautiful California was like a dream. "I just hope transferring my parole won't be too much of a problem."

"I don't know why it would," Kayne said.

"Don't worry about that. You just worry about picking out that wedding dress, baby. You're going to California, and you're going to start all over and be happy. I won't let anything stand in your way." My mother smiled proudly.

"Thank you, Mommy. I love you."

"I love you, too, baby. Everything's going to work out. You deserve this."

Chapter 17

Tuesday—October 17, 2006

Kayne had gone on several overnight runs with Chris, who I hadn't talked to since his crazy baby mama trashed my truck and he came out of pocket to fix it. Knowing full well that he was a snake, I could only imagine his reason for agreeing to repair the damage so quickly. He knew I wasn't going to leave Kayne. He also knew if he even looked at me sideways Kayne would be all over his ass. Whatever his reason, I realized that I never thanked him, especially since he brought my truck back with some improvements—26" rims and TVs in the headrests.

At home after another boring day at work, I curled up on the bed, looked at the phone and decided to call Chris before I forgot. I picked up the receiver and pressed *67. The last thing I wanted was for him to get my house num-

her. Friend or not, Kayne was not hearing Chris calling me at the crib now that he was basically living with me.

"Hello?" a female voice answered with attitude.

"Can I speak to Chris please?" I asked politely.

"He ain't here right now. He left his phone with me. Who is this?"

"Who is this?" I asked, catching the same attitude she already had. I was hoping it was his baby mama.

"Shalauna," she replied. "If you want me to let him know you called, I need to know your name."

"Just tell him it's Mina with a message from Kayne."

"Mina, as in the bitch who went nuts over Kayne and got sent to the looney bin?"

"No, Mina as in Kayne's down-ass chick who knows where you live and feels no way about coming over there to beat your ass." I felt my blood boiling. How dare she bring up me being locked up. Was my business a damn joke? This trick was trying to punk me.

"Well, Mina, you might not have heard the news, but Kayne ain't yours no more. Guess you weren't allowed visitors or letters while you were in isolation. Things done changed. Kayne is getting married to my cousin. They have a brand new baby boy, so sweetie, I suggest you get your mind right and stop chasing a man that don't want your crazy ass."

"Oh, I see you want to be a bad ass now, but where was all this gangsta when you cried to the Feds after they ran in your house?" I could hear Shalauna gasp. "I don't know who you think you fucking with, but Mina is back. Kayne is mine and anyone who thinks otherwise will get laid out."

"I knew Kayne wasn't shit," Shalauna whispered. I could tell she was thinking of how she was going to break the news to Marla, and more importantly, find out where I was.

"Talk shit about my man again, bitch, and you *and* Marla can and will get it."

"I didn't tell you my cousin's name was Marla," said a stunned Shalauna.

"I know everything." With that, I hung up the phone. I had already wasted too much time playing telephone games with her. Now I had to do my counting exercises and calm my nerves. I hadn't been this heated in months. It wasn't even because she tried to call me out on being crazy. It was the fact that I was on the phone with the dumb bitch who snitched and put my Kayne in jail. I did so much to try to get him out. I would have done his time for him and in essence, I did, but then she opened her mouth and he ended up behind bars. He and I had both wasted too many years apart.

Hungry from all the arguing, I headed to the kitchen to cook dinner. As I was placing the spaghetti in the boiling water, the phone rang.

"Hey," I answered as cheerfully as possible, seeing that it was Marla on the Caller ID. I was surprised it had taken her this long to call me. I had been off the phone with Shalauna for over ten minutes.

"Keon's cheating on me!" Marla was frantic and breathing all heavy like she just ran a marathon. Isaiah was crying his head off in the background.

"What?" I faked concern.

"My cousin just called and told me that some chick called claiming she was Keon's ex." I liked how she so conveniently left out the part about me calling Chris' phone. I guess she thought "Mya" was still seeing him so why get me upset?

"Who is this chick? Did she give a name?"

"Mina!" Marla yelled. "The bitch's name is Mina. My cousin says it's the same chick who was with Keon before he got locked up. I asked her if the girl could just be some dummy playing on the phone, and she told me this girl knew too much."

"What did your cousin say she said?" I wanted to see if my message got lost in translation.

"That's besides the point, Mya," she snapped. Marla was loyal, and she wasn't about to spill the beans about her cousin snitching. "My life is over. I can never compete with that girl. All these years, he would never tell me anything about her—not even her name. I tried to find out who she was and just when I thought my life was good—I got a baby, I'm engaged she comes back, calling my cousin on the phone no less."

"Marla, girl, calm down. Go get your baby. You're forgetting you have someone else to take care of. Fuck a nigga who wants to cheat. You got that little boy to take care of. Did you even call Kayne about all this? She could be lying, you know."

"I just tried to call him before I called you. His phone is going straight to voicemail. I bet he's with that bitch right now."

"He isn't with her." I knew that because he wasn't with me. "You need to calm down."

"Yeah, you know, you right. I'm going to wait until he comes home, and I'll get to the bottom of this." I could hear her pick up the baby, who was now cooing into the phone. "Mya, thanks for calming me down. I was about to go crazy in here. Do you think you can come over?"

"I'm sorry, Marla, I can't. I'm in the middle of cooking. My mother is coming over for dinner."

"Oh, okay." She sounded hurt.

"Look, we'll get together soon. Remember, Marla, you are a smart, beautiful woman." I couldn't believe I was saying the words that were coming out of my mouth. I turned my emotions off and kept the positive words flowing. I was probably repeating some shit I heard on Dr. Phil. "You deserve much more than this. If Keon doesn't respect you after all you've done for him then leave him. However, there is always a chance that the chick is lying, and the last thing you want to do is accuse him of something he isn't doing. The moment you do that the trust is gone." I listened to my words and realized that even though I was in the middle of all this bullshit and had stolen Kayne right from under Marla's nose, Kayne trusted me, and I trusted him.

"Thanks, Mya. Let me get in here and feed this baby. But I need to tell you this. I know we haven't known each other long, but I really appreciate you."

"Marla, that's what friends are for. We'll talk more later."

"Thanks, Mya. Later."

I hung up and rested against the kitchen island. This shit was draining me. It wasn't supposed to be taking a toll on me, but it was. I just wanted to get my man back, break a couple of windows and slash some tires, not become my enemy's best friend and shoulder to cry on. Where the hell was Kayne? I needed to dump this emotional baggage on him. Fuck, I wasn't even hungry anymore. I turned off the pots and went to bed.

With my conscience starting to weigh heavily on me, I called Kelly.

"Hey, girl!" She was driving with the music blasting and sounded like she was in a good mood.

"Turn that down."

"Okay." She did as I said. "What's the matter with you?"

"I don't think I can do this anymore."

"Do what?"

"This whole revenge thing. I just got off the phone with Marla. Long story, but basically she knows that Kayne is with me."

"She knows he is with who? Mina or Mya? I can't keep up with all your personalities these days," she laughed.

"Kelly, it's not funny," I whined, trying not to crack a smile myself. "Marla knows that Kayne is back with Mina, but she doesn't know that I'm Mina."

"Okay, isn't that what you wanted? I know cold-hearted killer over there ain't gettin' soft on me."

"Hell no." I perked up.

"Okay then, you got her right where you want her. You can't switch the game up now. Since when did you start

caring about her feelings?"

"Nah, it's not even like that." I tried to downplay my moment of weakness. "I was just joking with you, girl."

"Yeah, okay. Well, let me go. I'm pulling into my driveway now. Zelle and I are going to the movies tonight. I'll catch up with you later."

"A'ight."

I managed to doze off for what seemed like an hour, but when I was awakened by my cell phone ringing, I looked at the clock and saw I was only out for fifteen minutes. "Hello?" I answered, half asleep.

"Hey, did you call me?"

"Yeah, I just wanted to call and say thanks for getting my car back looking brand new." I wasn't going to bring up Shalauna if he wasn't. Who knew, he might have been dealing with her on the side and didn't want me to know. Why else would she be answering his cell?

"You're welcome. It's the least I could do." He sounded sincerely apologetic.

"It was crazy, I have to admit. But there are definitely no hard feelings."

"Alright, *Mya*." He laughed.

"My secret is still safe with you, right?"

"You know it, baby girl. I don't know what you got up your sleeve, but I definitely ain't no snitch." I wondered if he knew he was dealing one-on-one with a snitch.

"Thanks."

"Plus, I got your back. Speaking of which, I would love to see that back, front and middle again. When you gonna let me take you out again, get us a hotel and shit? We can

finish what we started last time."

I knew it! Nigga was trying to be all nice like he gave a damn. Dudes will do anything for some pussy. In Chris' case, it was dropping dough to fix my car and covering for my lying ass. "Ha, I'm gonna have to get back to you on that one," I lied. "Kayne has been playing me close. I'd have to sneak away to see you or wait till he goes out of town."

"I understand. Kayne can be a little on the clingy side. I used to tell him to ease off of me when we were locked up. Nigga always wanted me to protect him."

"Well, I gotta go." I wasn't about to get into yet another argument with someone lying about my man. I had enough. Before he could say another word, I pressed the *End* button.

* * * *

"Heard you been in here playing on phones," Kayne said as he walked into the bedroom and lay across my lap. "And why is there a pot of soggy spaghetti on the stove?"

"I totally forgot about that. If you hungry, I suggest you order something. While you at it, order me something, too. I just got my appetite back."

"Chinese good?"

"Yeah."

"So." Kayne got up to get the menu from the kitchen. "What up with the telephone games?" he yelled from the hall.

"Huh?" I acted like I didn't hear.

"I got like five voicemail messages from Marla talking about, 'Who the fuck is Mina?' and how you called her cousin." He walked back in the bedroom and sat down on the edge of the bed.

"She's lying. I called Chris."

Kayne looked up from the menu. "What you call that nigga for?"

"I called to thank him for fixing my car, and Shalauna answered the phone." He was visibly mad now. "Baby, wait before you lose it, it's not even like that. That bitch is crazy. She wanted to know who I was. I couldn't tell her Mya, well I could have, but hell, I wanted her to know that she was talking to the woman she took you away from."

"Mina, I can't even go there with you right now. I'm hungry. Whatever you did I know you are smart enough to know not to blow our shit up. So I guess Marla is tight now?"

"Oh, she called me, and I calmed her down. Told her not to jump to conclusions and blah, blah, blah." We both laughed.

"Mina, I love you, but you a mess. Remind me to never cross you. You just straight venom."

"Baby, don't stress." I started rubbing his shoulders. "Everything is going to work out perfectly. You and me together, who can stop us?"

"We need a vacation." Kayne stretched his neck, enjoying the massage I was giving him.

"That would be nice," I said, imagining hot sex on a beach.

"Yeah? That's why I'm taking you to the Smoky Mountains for your birthday."

"Baby, are you serious?"

"You know I am." He looked up at me, smiling.

"Thank you, baby. I can't wait!"

Chapter 18

Tuesday—November 7, 2006

Kayne woke me up bright and early by kissing me on the neck. When I opened my eyes, he was standing there with a dozen red roses and a small box with the most perfect bow I'd ever seen. It was almost too pretty to rip open.

"Happy birthday, baby!"

"Aww, thank you." I sat up in the bed with the biggest smile on my face. I was finally twenty-one. If you looked at the life I lived, you would have thought I was much older than I was. The first time I spent a birthday with Kayne, I turned eighteen. The big celebration then was that I was no longer a minor. I remember how happy we both were to make our relationship public without fear of him getting arrested for statutory rape. We spent the week in Puerto Rico and I never thought another birthday could top that

one, but the day was off to a great start.

"What's that?" I asked, pointing to the box that he laid in my lap.

"Open it." He nudged the box closer to me, placed the roses on the nightstand and took a seat next to me. I tugged on the ribbon and the bow unraveled. I opened the black velvet box to reveal a stunning tennis bracelet.

"Kayne ..." my jaw dropped.

"Here," he said, reaching for my hand. "Let me help you put it on."

"It's beautiful." I admired the bracelet along with my engagement ring, which I hadn't taken off.

"Hurry up, get out the bed. We need to hit the road." Kayne had made plans for us to visit Gatlinburg, Tennessee for four days.

"I'm coming, baby. Let me take a quick shower. All the bags are in the living room. You can load the car. I won't be long, I promise."

I slept for two hours in the car and stayed up the last four to keep Kayne company. As we turned into the Legacy Resort Chalet, I was amazed at how beautiful it was. The fall sun beamed off the mountains, capped with snow. Stepping out of the car, the brisk air recharged me. The leaves were all shades of brown and red. I had been stuck in the city so long I forgot that there was a world outside of my window. Kayne slammed the trunk of the car, snapping me out of my daydream.

"It's your day, baby, so what do you want to do?" We were inside of our cottage, which was decorated like something out of a Martha Stewart magazine. "We can go out to eat tonight, or I can cook for you. I brought food to put on the grill," Kayne said, opening a cooler inside.

I turned on the TV in the living room and collapsed on the soft leather couch. "Baby, you know I love your cooking. We can stay here and celebrate. You're all I need today." I smiled as he leaned over the couch to kiss me. "What did you bring to grill?"

"Some steaks, shrimp, salmon and corn. We can go to the store and get anything else you want."

"Ooh, that sounds good. I'm getting hungry already. Let's go pick up some stuff for a salad. I'll make it, and let's make some margaritas, too."

After everything was done, we sat down at the dining room table to eat together.

"Thank you for bringing me here, baby. You always know how to make my birthday special."

"Only the best for my baby."

"I love it. It's beautiful here." I walked out onto the deck. "Looking over the mountains is like being in a dream."

"Fall is the perfect time to come here." Kayne walked up behind me and rested his head on my shoulder, kissing my neck.

"So, Mr. NaCore, what are we going to do tomorrow?" Our picture perfect moment was interrupted by his cell phone ringing and vibrating in his pocket. "Who is it?" My eyes were fixed on the country skyline. There was no need for me to look at his face because I knew who it was. Kayne quickly pressed the *Ignore* button, sending the call to voicemail.

"You know who. Fuck her. I'm here with the woman I love."

"Whatever." I rolled my eyes, irritated that Marla was calling him. Suddenly my phone rang from inside the house. Kayne looked at me with a smirk. I rolled my eyes and went to answer it. I'd be damned if she was going to blow up my phone all night.

"Hello?" I answered.

"Happy birthday!" Marla sang.

"Thank you." I tried to match her excitement, but she had me beat.

"What do you have planned for the day?"

"I'm in Tennessee with my mom and her boyfriend."

"That sounds like fun."

"Yeah, it's a nice little getaway since I can't be with my boo."

"Aww, I've been there, girl. Luckily, Keon and I are doing much better." I felt her smile come through the phone. I rolled my eyes. "Great, well, I just wanted to call and wish you a happy birthday. Have fun, and I'll see you whenever you get back."

"Okay, I'll talk to you later."

"Who was that?" Kayne asked sarcastically.

"Marla. She just called to wish me a happy birthday." I walked past him to the kitchen to pour another glass of wine. "I told her that I would call her back after I finished making love to *her man*, Keon," I teased.

"Is that so?" He played along.

"Yep."

Kayne walked up to me and put his arms around my

waist. "So what she say after that?"

"She told me to tell you to call her afterward." We both laughed.

"Anyway, like I was saying before we were interrupted, I got a surprise for you tomorrow. Then we can go shopping if you want. There are a lot of outlets around here. I was thinking Thursday we could go to the amusement park, Dollywood. It's all up to you."

"I haven't been on a roller coaster since I was thirteen. That sounds like fun. Let's do everything you just said, that is, if we can get out of bed."

"Oh, before we go there, I got something else for you. Sit down." Kayne motioned toward the barstool at the counter. "Close your eyes."

"Why?"

"Mina, close your eyes."

"I love it when you get bossy," I joked, covering my eyes with my hands. I heard Kayne walk out of the kitchen and back in, but after that, I heard nothing. Momentarily, I could feel Kayne standing next to me.

"Okay, open them."

Before me was an adorable miniature cake with the number twenty-one and *Happy Birthday Amina* written on top. I blew out the candles and made a wish. Then I used my finger and dipped it into the icing, feeding it to Kayne, who licked it off. We each fed each other cake and decided to take the action to the outside hot tub.

"I can't wait to see the surprise tomorrow." I kissed Kayne as I sat on his lap, both of us engulfed in the warm, bubbly water.

"You're going to love it. I already know."

"As much as I love you?" I asked, kissing him again.

"I don't know if you could love anything else more than me." He smiled.

"Me either." His phone began ringing again. It was inside and neither one of us were going to get out of the water to get it. Besides, we knew it had to be Marla.

"When we get out, the first thing you're gonna do is turn that phone off. I don't want her ruining my birthday trip by being a bug-a-boo the whole time. And just so you know, that Young Jeezy ring tone is very annoying." I rolled my eyes while getting up to get out of the water. Kayne grabbed me, pulling me back down on his lap.

"Nothing is going to ruin this trip," he said, getting out of the water and grabbing the towels for us. "You ready to get out and go finish this birthday off right?"

"Lead the way." On the way inside he fished inside of his pants pockets and pulled out his cell phone. The melodic tone alerted both of us that it was now turned off.

In the bedroom, he laid me across the bed and lit candles around the room. Ne-Yo's CD was on repeat. Every ounce of anger I had about Marla was gone by the time he placed his lips on my skin. He worked his way up from my feet to my neck. Four hours later, I went to sleep exhausted, but after sleeping for six hours, I woke up feeling refreshed. After getting dressed in something comfortable but cute, Kayne took me to breakfast at The Pancake Pantry. His big surprise: an hour helicopter ride that covered ninety miles of the beautiful Tennessee mountains.

"I never would have guessed in a million years we would

be flying over the mountains!" I exclaimed as I snapped pictures and caught as much as I could on video.

"Yeah, this is nice, ain't it? Makes you feel like you on top of the world." He smiled.

"We are on top of the world, baby." I truly felt as if we were.

After landing, we drove to Pigeon Forge to shop at the Belz Factory, which featured eighty-five name brand outlets. I literally shopped until I dropped. We went back to the Chalet to change clothes and go eat dinner at Lineberger's Seafood Company. The food was great. To end our evening, Kayne and I cuddled in the bed where we watched half of a movie before we were both out cold.

* * * *

The next morning we woke up to go to Dollywood, where we spent five whole hours feeling like kids again. I wanted to spend our last night in, so we picked up dinner and took it back to the Chalet. Before retreating to the hot tub, I remembered there was something I wanted to show Kayne.

"Baby, come here," I called out to him, sitting down on the bed. I handed him a small photo album.

"What's this? Kayne began looking through the album.

"They're pictures from our trip to Puerto Rico," I told him. "You never got a chance to see them."

Kayne sat quietly as he looked at each photo. He seemed nostalgic when he put the book down. Kayne looked at me. "I love you, Amina, and nothing will ever tear us apart again … ever."

I didn't realize the pictures would have that effect on him. "Come on, Kayne, let's go get into the Jacuzzi."

"So was this trip as good as Puerto Rico?" Kayne inquired as he lay between my legs in the tub.

"Even better. I had the time of my life. This was so special because we're together again, and it's something about the mountains that just turns me on." I purred, licking his ear.

"It's something about you that turns me on, too." He turned around to kiss me on the lips, then my neck, and down to both of my nipples. He sucked them gently as he played with my clit underneath the hot water. I grabbed his dick, stroking it as we both made each other moan in ecstasy. Finally, I placed his dick inside of me, demanding that he make love to me slow and steady. Hearing the warm water softly splash while our bodies clung to one another, I never wanted him to stop. After the water turned cold, I got out and turned the heat back up, then begged him to do it again and again. Finally when I couldn't take any more, he washed my body. When I got out of the tub, he gave me a hot oil massage on the king-sized bed. I fell asleep to his touch, and I was still amazed at how he had managed to make my eighteenth and twenty-first birthdays the best I'd ever had.

Chapter 19

Thanksgiving Day, 2006

I was on my way over to Zelle and Kelly's for dinner when Marla called to invite me to her house. I told her I might be able to make it later that night, but had no plans to stop by. She was still living in a fantasy world where Keon was hers and they would soon be married. Kayne went over to see the baby from time to time, but little did she know, her so-called fiancé was living with me. He admitted that he hadn't called off the wedding with her yet, but told her he needed some time alone after finding out about Jason. I was somewhat skeptical at first about him even seeing her until I accepted that it was all a part of the plan. We would get her and Shalauna back soon enough.

When I arrived at Zelle's house, I couldn't wait to dig into the meal of smoked turkey, macaroni and cheese,

yams, collard greens, corn bread, dressing and sweet potato pies that Kelly, Shayna and I had prepared the night before. After the full house of guests gathered to pray over the delicious meal, everyone began eating. Kayne showed up a few minutes late, coming from Marla's. My mother and Gary came for dessert because they ate with Gwen and my grandmother at Gary's house. As everyone sat around mingling, Shayna decided it was the perfect time to make her surprise announcement. She stood with a smile in front of the full dining room.

"I just want to say to everyone here that this is a beautiful Thanksgiving, and I'm thrilled to be here with everyone who has become my family. I also have an announcement to make." She paused, smiling at Damen, who sat next to her holding her hand. "*We* have an announcement to make. Damen and I will be the proud parents of a baby girl in April."

"Are you serious?" I asked aloud as everyone clapped excitedly. I couldn't believe I was getting a baby sister. I was thrilled. Looking at her closely in the loose-fitting shirt she was wearing, I didn't know how I hadn't realized she was disguising her pudge.

"Yes! I found out it was a girl right before we came to Cincinnati."

"Daddy, I'm going to have a baby sister? I'm so happy for you two," I said, getting up to give them both a big hug.

"Thank you, baby," Damen said, squeezing me tight. "I'm glad she'll have someone to look up to and show her the ropes."

"I might just steal her from you and take her with me

and Kayne to California." I had let my tongue get ahead of me.

"California?" Damen looked at me, confused.

"Well, I guess I should make my announcement now." I stood in front of everyone and Kayne stood by my side. "Kayne and I are engaged, and we're moving to California!"

Everyone looked shocked but happy. Kelly damn near jumped through the roof as she rushed over to hug us both.

Shayna was almost as excited as Kelly. "Amina, that's great! We need to get started on the wedding plans right away! Have you talked about when you want to have it and where?"

"We've thought about a small beach wedding in California, near our condo, most likely in the summer."

"Oh my God, yes! That would be gorgeous, Mina," Kelly squealed excitedly.

Damen looked worried and so did Zelle. Neither one of them said anything.

"Speaking of good news, Gary and I also have an announcement." My mother caught Damen's look and tried to lighten the mood. "Markus' attempted murder trial begins this Monday, so please keep us in your prayers."

"Definitely," Damen said, giving Gary a respectful nod.

"That's great, and I'll pray for the best, Ms. K," Kelly said. "Ms. K" was a nickname Kelly had been calling my mother since childhood. The ladies began clearing empty plates from the table.

"Thanks, sweetie," my mother told her, getting up to go to the kitchen.

Damen, Zelle and Kayne went into the living room

where I knew they would have a deep discussion about the engagement. Gary stayed at the table with Canoray, who held a good conversation for a three-year-old.

"You know, Damen's probably a little shocked, but I know he's happy for you, Amina, and so am I," Shayna admitted, giving me another hug in the kitchen. My mother smiled. She seemed to admire Shayna's sweet nature.

"I'm happy for her, too. I just really think a new atmosphere will be the best for Amina," my mother explained to Shayna. "And did she tell you she's planning on getting a business degree and opening up a bookstore?" My mother beamed.

"No! Amina, sweetie, that's wonderful! I'm so proud of you! Come here and give me another hug!" She embraced me tightly. "I'm just so overjoyed to see you happy and doing well."

"Thank you, Shayna."

"Girl, a bookstore? That's what's up for real! Get that money!" Kelly was just as excited. "I'm going to miss you so much Mina, but you know I'm excited for you. I can't believe you're going to be an old married lady," she teased.

"Thanks for being happy for me and being there during the hard times. I love you all. You're my family and really all I have. I appreciate each one of you so much," I told them.

Damen came in the kitchen and asked to speak to me in the living room.

"Yes, Daddy?" I gave him my little girl look. Kayne and Zelle sat silent.

"I want to let you know I'm happy for you and Kayne, and I've given him my blessing." I couldn't hide my huge

smile. "But, I want you two to take things slow and be smarter this time around. I'm proud of the progress you've made so far, and I'm also proud of Kayne, who has made plans to take care of you the proper way. " He glanced at Kayne, who smiled back. I'm sure hearing that from Damen felt like winning the lottery after years of Damen's disapproval. "I know he'll take care of you, but I want you to know you'll always be my baby girl, and whenever you need me I'll always be there, because I'll always be Daddy. I've also spoken with Kayne and told him that I want to pay for the wedding and honeymoon, wherever you choose to go." He gave me the smile I was waiting for.

"Daddy, thank you so much! I promise I won't make things too expensive. I really just want a small wedding." I hugged him, ecstatic about having his approval.

"Nothing's too extravagant for my baby girl. You know that, so get started on the plans."

"I will as soon as possible. I've got so much to think about!" I couldn't control my excitement.

"I want to wish you and Kayne the best. I love you, little sis." Zelle got up to hug me.

"I love you, too, thanks." Everything was so perfect. I wondered if heaven could compare. I told Zelle and Damen about my plan to start school and eventually open my own business. I had never seen my father look so proud of me. He and Zelle promised to be there to help along the way, and I knew with them and the rest of my family backing me, that all of my dreams would come true sooner than I hoped.

Chapter 20

Thursday—December 14, 2006

December had arrived with winter weather to match, and I was already in the holiday spirit. Kayne and I had purchased a small Christmas tree for the living room and decorated it with white and gold ornaments. I hung decorations all over the house and turned my condo into our own winter wonderland. The weatherman on the morning news was saying the high for the day would be 35 degrees with a chance of snow. I turned off the TV and rolled back into Kayne's arms. If only I could have stayed there forever. Just as I was contemplating calling off of work, I perked up and headed for the shower.

Today was Marla's first day back from maternity leave. Although she was coming back, I wouldn't see her nearly as much because she would be returning to her nursing posi-

tion the next week. Before leaving the house, I decided I was going to take her to lunch to keep things smooth so as not to leave any suspicions.

"Girl, it seems like you've been gone forever. Are you happy to be going back to your old job?" Under the table, I slipped my engagement ring off and placed it in my purse. I had gotten so used to not seeing Marla that I forgot to take it off. From now on, I was going to have to leave it at home. I couldn't risk her seeing it and asking me questions.

"You mean happy not being able to sit on my ass anymore?" We both laughed. "I have something for you." She pulled out a small gift box from her purse.

"Girl, what is this?" I asked excitedly, unwrapping the red wrapping paper.

"Just a little Christmas gift."

"Oops, did you want me to wait to open it?"

"No, go ahead open it now." She looked on.

"Okay." I continued to unwrap, eventually uncovering a small picture frame ornament with the letter *M* engraved at the top. It had a picture of us in it from the senior family picnic. "This is so cute. I just put up my tree, and it will be perfect. Thanks, Marla, that was really sweet. I love little stuff like this." I really did like the tasteful ornament, but I was tossing the picture as soon as I got home, or maybe I'd put it on the tree and see if Kayne caught it.

"You're welcome. I saw it and thought it was so cute. I just had to get it for you, and since we have the same initial, it fit with the picture, Marla and Mina."

"Who?" I looked at her in shock.

"Oh, I'm sorry, girl." She looked out the window with

concern in her eyes.

"I know you been gone for a few months, but how you forget my name?" I joked.

"Mya, girl, my mind has been all over the place."

"Who is Mina?" It took everything in me not to give up the secret 'cause I was about tired of the whole façade.

"That's the girl who has Keon." She turned to me with tears in her eyes. "Everything is all messed up. Ever since she called, Keon has been cold, and honestly, he hasn't been home in weeks. He'll come to drop off stuff for the baby, but that's it."

This wasn't news to me. Well, the dropping stuff off was news, but if the kid was his I'd rather he take care of the little bastard than not. I couldn't be mad at that. Caught up in my own thoughts, I felt Marla staring at me for a response. "Sweetie," I sprung into caring friend mode, "this is the answer you needed. Maybe it's time you move on." If I could get her to move on from Kayne on her own then the hurt wouldn't be as bad for her. Homegirl was starting to come apart, and I was worried she was going to lose it. I know I shouldn't have cared, especially since things were going according to plan, but damn.

"No, no, Mya, I can't move on," she whispered. "I have to get him back!" She slammed her fist on the table, making me jump back and catching attention from nearby tables. "Will you help me?"

"Help you how?" There was definitely a limit to how much I was willing to do to make her believe I was her friend.

"I need to find this Mina bitch."

"Oh, well—"

"Can you ask around and see who might know her?" she interrupted me.

"Marla, I don't know anyone really. I just moved here to get away from drama. Remember, my man is locked up and where we used to live there are hundreds of chicks who want to come after me because they think my man is theirs. I told myself that I wasn't chasing after no girls or fighting over a man, not just my man, but any man." I could tell she was not happy with what I had to say. "Look, you're a mother now. What are you gonna do if you find this girl? What if she was just someone playing around? Has she ever called back?"

"No." She hung her head down in shame.

"How do you know that she's even the reason Keon is gone? What if it's because he isn't sure about the baby being his? You said it yourself, even you aren't sure." Obviously, I had touched a nerve because right then Marla began sobbing. The waitress interrupted her antics with our food.

"Is there anything else I can bring you ladies?" She looked over at Marla like she was crazy.

"No, thank you. We're fine." After she walked away I got up and moved to Marla's side of the booth to sit next to her. "Girl, you can't be losing it like this. Not here. Dry those tears. Don't cry over no man. Now, let's eat our lunch, and we'll talk about this later." I got up and went back to my seat, looking around to see if I knew anyone in the restaurant.

"So what are your plans for Christmas?" I quickly

changed the subject.

"I think I'm going to cook a big dinner. You're welcome to come over since you didn't get a chance to make it over for Thanksgiving."

"I'd love to, but I'm flying out to Long Beach to visit my family for a few days," I lied, simply to avoid her invitation.

"Oh really? Keon's mother lives in Long Beach. I have a few relatives in LA, too. Did Donna give you some time off? She can be funny acting around Christmas, I'm telling you."

"Yeah, I'll get Christmas Eve up until the 27th off."

"That's good. You should have a beautiful Christmas out there. I wish I could escape this weather."

"Girl, who you telling? It's getting ridiculous, and they're talking about more snow soon."

"Yeah, I hate cold weather. If I had the chance, I would love to move to Cali. I even talked to Keon about it a few times," Marla gushed, lying as usual. Although she never said, I knew the reason she was just now getting back from maternity leave was because she was busy chasing Jason around. She was trying to get him back since Kayne was never around. Originally, she was supposed to be back to work around Thanksgiving.

"I was so excited about the baby's first Christmas and spending it as a family, but the way things are looking, I don't think that's going to happen."

"Marla, girl, please don't get yourself worked up over this again. I don't have any more Kleenex in my purse," I joked to keep the mood light, but really I was about two seconds away from stabbing her crying ass with my knife.

"Mya, I left something out."

"What?"

"Somehow, Keon found out about Jason. He won't tell me how, but he says he wants a paternity test, or we can't get married." I had no idea Kayne hadn't shown her the pictures. "I refuse to give him one. I mean, if he can't tell me how he knows about me cheating, why should I give him a test?"

"Did you admit to it?"

"Well, at first I played dumb, but then I figured that would get me absolutely nowhere. So I told him Jason and I had a one night stand, and of course that's a lie. I just saw Jason last night, but it doesn't even matter because it's enough for him not to trust me anymore."

"The best thing to do is just get the test, Marla. It's something you'll eventually have to face if you want to be with Keon. You just have to pray for the best."

She put her head down to hide her tears. "Mya, Jason has already cut me off. He told me even if Isaiah is his, he doesn't want anything to do with him. And Mya, last night he told me he's bisexual." She wiped her pitiful eyes. An alarm sounded in my head that drowned out everything else around me. If Kayne was sleeping with this dirty chick with no condom he could have exposed me to Jason's nasty dick.

"Mya, are you okay?"

"Yeah, girl, I'm sorry. That's just some heavy shit. Are you alright?"

"No, not really. I just can't imagine the things Jason was doing behind my back. The thought disgusts me. I think I

seriously need an HIV test, considering the circumstances."

I felt like passing out onto the floor.

"If you're feeling like that you need to get that shit done ASAP!"

"I will. Please pray for me, Mya."

"I definitely will." I was going to pray for myself even more.

Chapter 21

Christmas Day, 2006

The entire living room was covered with opened gift boxes and torn wrapping paper. Each of us had bought the other the exact same thing—clothes and shoes. I was upset because Kayne bought me the cutest pair of Manolo sandals, but I'd have to wait months to wear them. So I decided to wear them around the house and even gave him a fashion show of all the sexy outfits he bought me. He even joined in the fun, showing off the Sean John suit I got him. After an hour of that, Kayne decided to make us some hot chocolate.

I excused myself and walked toward the bathroom. Once inside, I found the EPT that I had purchased earlier in the week. I knew that whatever the results were, they could shape our future. What would be a better present for the both of us than to find out we were going to be parents? I didn't want him to know I was taking it in the event that it was a false alarm. Although my period was three weeks late, I didn't want to get his hopes high.

"Mina, do you want marshmallows in yours?" Kayne yelled from the kitchen, startling me, as I peed on the stick.

"Uh, yeah, baby. That's fine." I dried off and placed the test on the side of the tub. When I walked back into the living room, Kayne was waiting for me on the couch.

"Everything okay?"

"Yeah, I was just using the bathroom." I nestled up next to him on the couch. "I was thinking, all of these gifts are nice, but nothing is better than this right here, us sitting on the couch in each other's arms. We getting married, Kayne. Can you believe that?" He laughed. Thugs didn't show too much excitement, so I had to be giddy for the both of us.

"What time we headed to your mother's house for dinner?"

"I told her six. Why?"

"I wanted to drop some stuff over at Marla's for Isaiah." I turned around to face him. "Look, until we get that test done there is a chance he's mine. I ain't going to stay long, just see how he's doing, drop off these gifts and come back here."

"Whatever." There was no need to start a fight. Just then I remembered my own test results. "Excuse me," I said, getting up from his embrace.

"Mina, where you going? Come on, don't get upset over

this. We're having a nice time, enjoying Christmas."

"I'm not mad, Kayne," I said without turning around. "I have to go to the bathroom."

Once inside, I closed the door behind me, sat on the closed toilet and took a moment before I looked at the results. Either my life was going to be changed forever and Kayne and I would be starting a family or I'd just have to be happy with what I had now. Slowly, I reached for the pregnancy test and saw two lines. I grabbed the box to make sure what I was seeing was correct. It was. I was pregnant! Overcome with happiness, the tears flowed.

I thought back to '03 when I took my first pregnancy test and discovered I was pregnant. I took the circumstances for what they were and embraced the fact that I was going to become someone's mother. After I lost my baby, I was mad at God for so long, but with Him, I understood timing was everything. When I saw two lines appear, I knew God was telling me now was the time. I began shedding tears right there in the bathroom. Tears of joy that washed away the tears of pain. Kayne opened the door and came in.

"What's the matter, baby?" He looked confused and concerned.

"Nothing, baby, I'm just happy that's all," I said, drying my eyes, still holding the test stick behind my back.

"I'm happy, too." He pulled me close, kissing me.

"I have a surprise for you," I whispered into his ear.

"Oh yeah? What's that?" He kissed me again.

"Look." I handed him the results.

"Does this mean what I think it means?" he asked with

a puzzled look.

"What do you think it means?"

"That my soon-to-be wife is having my baby?" He was smiling ear to ear.

"Yep, you guessed right!"

"I love you." He kissed my lips again. "I love you, too." He bent to my belly and kissed it softly, then picked me up and set me on the sink.

As he slid my red and black lace gown up around my waist, I wrapped my legs tightly around him, pulling him toward me. I instantly became soaking wet after feeling his hardness searching for its home, awakening every emotion in my body. When he was finally where I wanted him to be, I grinded my hips toward him, gradually picking up speed as he pushed himself into me deeper and deeper. Pulling down my gown straps, he licked and sucked each of my nipples. I began moaning as I watched him and continued to throw my pussy to him. Only seconds before he came inside of me, my pussy throbbed tightly while my hot wetness dripped slowly down his dick.

* * * *

Kayne drank his hot chocolate as we lay in the bed together discussing wedding plans. The date was set for Saturday, July 7th in sunny California. His cousin Quinn was deep into the real estate game out there and owned a beach front property where he agreed to let us have our wedding and reception. We both wanted a small wedding. Zelle had already been asked to be the Best Man, and of

course Kelly would be my Maid of Honor. Kayne decided on the colors. He wanted to wear peach and white tuxes with peach Gators. I instantly decided on a certain peach-colored Prada dress that I had seen in a magazine for the bridesmaids, who were going to be Shayna, Butter and Trina. I had spoken to Trina on Christmas Eve. She was so excited to hear about the wedding, and I was equally happy to hear that she would soon be graduating from Florida A&M with a bachelor's in Psychology. She planned to go on to get her master's. I told her if I ever went crazy again, I would be sure to hire her as my shrink.

I was also proud of Butter, who was working on getting clean. She was currently doing a 30-day program at the CCAT house. She said that Rome had told her he wanted to see his queen strong again. That was all it took for her to decide to make herself over. I knew addiction was a hard thing to overcome, but I prayed for Butter because I wanted to see her as the beautiful, strong woman I had always looked up to.

Kayne chose his cousin Quinn, along with Quinn's two other brothers, as groomsmen. Canoray was to be the ring bearer and Quinn's seven-year old daughter, India, would be the flower girl. Kayne showed me pictures of her, and she was beautiful. He planned to take me to Long Beach to meet his entire family in February. I couldn't wait.

"Baby, I'm going to be huge in July." I pictured myself seven months pregnant in a wedding dress. It was like a mini nightmare.

"I don't know about huge, but either way you're going to look beautiful." I gave him an unsure look. "What's that

look for? You don't believe me?"

"No, it's just that I pictured myself a certain way on my wedding day." I knew I probably sounded selfish.

"Well, picture yourself a different way, 'cause no matter what, you gotta carry my baby, and I can't wait a whole nine months to marry you. I already have to wait long enough."

"You always know what to say." I kissed him.

"So, are we keeping this a secret or you going to tell everybody?"

"I will when they start to notice." I laughed, looking forward to finding out who would be the first to realize I was expecting.

* * * *

After Kayne stopped by Marla's for an hour, I knew because I made him call me when he got there and when he left, he swung by the house to pick me up. We arrived at my mother's house at six thirty. When we walked in the door we were greeted by a full table of folks waiting on us so they could eat. Gary sat at the head, looking much better since the last time I'd seen him. Next to him was a seat for my mother. Gary's mother was sitting next to my mother and across from her were three seats for me and Kayne and my grandmother. I walked into the kitchen to help with the food.

"Here comes the bride." My grandmother put down the bowl of mashed potatoes and gave me a hug and kiss. "Well, where is he?" She helped me take off my coat and

walked me back to the dining room.

"Grandma, this is Keon NaCore, but we all call him Kayne. Kayne, this is my grandmother."

"Mrs. Perry. Nice to finally meet you." That comment made us both a little uncomfortable. My grandmother had heard only the worst about Kayne. Needless to say, she wasn't a fan of the man she thought turned her grandbaby onto the drug game. Seeing her welcome him either meant one of two things: she was losing her mind or she had finally gotten over her hatred for him. Besides, how could she not love Kayne once she saw him?

"Your mother told me the news. Congratulations, sweetheart. If this is the man who makes you happy, I'm happy for you," she said while looking at Kayne, who seemed a little uncomfortable standing next to the woman who tried her best to make me take a deal against him. I could tell that my grandmother was sincere. She could be very strict, but overall, she was a very loving and forgiving person.

"Thank you," Kayne said, then embraced her.

I smiled at him, letting him know everything was cool. We sat down to a delicious dinner of roast beef, mashed potatoes, my grandmother's green bean casserole and corn on the cob.

While Gary and Kayne talked in front of the TV, I discussed all of the details of the wedding with my mother, grandmother and Gary's mother. Before going back home, we stopped at Zelle's to drop off the trunk load of toys that I had for Canoray. He was so excited to see another load of gifts after already having opened dozens of toys from

Zelle and Kelly. I enjoyed seeing him rejoice over everything and began thinking that soon I would have my own child to spoil on Christmas. With that in mind, I almost spilled the beans to Kelly about being pregnant, but decided not to because I knew it would be more fun to make it a surprise.

Chapter 22

Sunday—February 11, 2007

Butter picked me up in a black Grand Am with tinted windows a little after eight o'clock. We were going to stake out Shalauna's house in Northside while Kayne made a run with Chris. Kayne was hesitant about me going at first, but Butter convinced him that I would be safe. She had a pistol on her, but she was sure nothing would happen. She wanted to watch the comings and goings of the spot before the final set up. The three of us were definitely cool with Shalauna and Chris getting popped, but if Butter saw any folks she knew coming in and out of there she was going to give them a heads up that the spot was hot. No use in innocent junkies getting locked up, too.

"When you see my car," Kayne said, "stay low. Niggas get 'noid when it's time to get some more shit and you just

never know who watchin.'"

"Alright, baby," I said as Kayne closed the door behind me.

"Butter, take care of my baby." Kayne was talking to us through the rolled down window.

"Man, I got this," laughed Butter. "Take yo' ass back upstairs. It's cold out here."

"Y'all be careful." He leaned through my window. "Call me when you get there."

"Okay, baby, I love you." I kissed him goodbye.

"Keep the windows rolled up," he said, overly worried.

"Why don't we start right now," Butter said, rolling up my window and giving Kayne his clue to leave.

Since we learned I was pregnant he'd been very protective of me. When I told him I was leaving to meet Butter downstairs, he jumped up from his PlayStation game, threw on some clothes and insisted on walking me downstairs. He said I might slip on the ice in the parking lot and hurt myself or the baby. As annoying as it was waiting the extra five minutes for him to get ready, it was also sweet.

During the short ride, Butter and I kept the mood light by talking about my favorite subject—the wedding. I had a craving for Starbucks on the way there, but of course I couldn't tell Butter that I was pregnant, so I made up some excuse for us to stop. So far I'd been lucky, no morning sickness, but I sure was getting cravings. Nachos with ice cream, pickles—oh, and I loved JELL-O for some reason.

We parked at the end of Shalauna's street where we had a pretty good view of her run-down house.

"Are we looking for anything in particular?" I asked

while snacking on a giant chocolate chip cookie.

"No, not really. I've been inside of that place more times than I can remember. We're here to see if traffic is light or heavy. That will tell us if Shalauna is a heavy weight or only dabbling. If word is out that she's the person to see, we should be seeing a parade of folks coming through here tonight. "

"So this is a stakeout," I laughed. "Feel like we should be taking pictures and eating donuts."

"Shit ain't that deep." Butter was focused on the task at hand.

I nodded in agreement just as I noticed a tan-colored Maxima pull into the driveway. Jason got out of the driver's seat while Marla got out of the passenger's side, and Shalauna emerged out of the back.

"Ain't this a bitch," I said, turning down the radio.

"What?" Butter was trying to figure out what I was looking at.

"Over there, the dude with Shalauna and that other chick, that's Marla. Just a few days ago, Marla was having a fit at lunch, talking about how much she loved Kayne, and here she is with the next dude."

"What you talking about?"

"That's dude who Marla was cheating on Kayne with. Shalauna swore up and down on the phone that her sweet cousin and Kayne were happy and in love, but she knew her cousin was a slut. Just look at that cheating bitch still with him!" I watched Jason smack Marla on the ass as they walked up the steps and into the house.

"They both got some nerve. If you ask me they're both

dumb hoes. Shalauna just got out of jail and is back at it, and Marla is getting flat out played while she think she's playing Kayne. Let me call him right now." I pulled my phone out of my purse. Kayne answered on the third ring, sounding like he had dozed off.

"What took you so long to call?"

"Guess who I'm looking at right now?" I was hyped.

"I hope it ain't the police."

"No, Kayne, Marla and Jason. They just got out of his car and they all boo'd up, holding hands and shit."

"I ain't even surprised, but I'm 'bout to roll through there shortly," Kayne said.

"He called you?"

"Yeah, sayin' we gotta make that run."

"Okay, cool." That meant they were going to see their supplier. "Kayne ..." I said, then paused. "Be careful, baby. This the same shit that got us locked up in the first place."

"I know, but this time, we're smarter. I'll see you tonight when I get home."

I closed my cell phone because Kayne ended the call.

"What he say?" Butter asked.

"Nothing. Where they go?" I asked, looking around in the darkness.

Shalauna opened the door, Jason and Marla kissed and went in behind her. "You just missed them go inside."

"Guess we'll just sit here and wait them out."

"Amina, I'm helping you and Kayne out because I know Shalauna and what she did to your man went against all the rules of the game. She deserves to be put under the jail for that and some other shady shit she done to some good folks

of mine, selling bad crack and whatnot to make a buck. Now Marla, I ain't got nothing bad to say about her, but I will say this." She turned to look me in the eyes. "You don't ever have to fight with a bitch over your man. Especially if you know he's your man. You feel me?"

"Yeah, I know Kayne is mine. I never expected this to go this far. When I got out of the mental institution, I came home and everything that I once had was gone. I went from counting stacks of cash in my bed to counting change as a sales clerk at The Shop. Everyone around had moved on. Kelly and my brother were playing house. Even my mother went and got herself a good man. I wanted that. I wanted to come home from a bullshit day at work and see my man. Most girls wouldn't dare go back to a man they went to prison for, but every day that I was in there, I could think of nothing else but my love for him.

"So when I came back home to my pathetic life, I saw him with Marla. She had what I thought was his heart, and I was miserable. Butter, all I wanted was my man back. Crazy thing is, I thought I was going to have to fight much harder than I did, but there's no going back now. After my run-in with Chris and Shalauna and seeing what a pathological liar Marla is, they deserve it."

"Girl, you know you a drama queen!" Butter laughed.

"Sometimes I regret posing as her friend though."

"Just know when it blows up, it will blow up big time. But you love Kayne, and you did what you had to do. I swear, Amina, you remind me so much of myself when I was younger. You may look at me now and see a junkie, but back then I was the baddest bitch in town. You couldn't even look at me sideways without getting smacked by one of Rome's henchmen," she said, getting animated. "I always had two of Rome's best men with me, you know, personal security."

"You had security guards? Who was kidnapping a black woman?" I laughed.

"You don't even know. The drug game was far worse then than it is now. Folks was disappearing on they way to the store and turning up dead in the gutter the next morning. Remember, everyone wanted to be Rome. As his lady, I got the most attention from chicks who wanted to take my spot and dudes who wanted to taste my spot." We chuckled at her silly joke. "Anyway, there was this one girl in particular. Actually, she was eight years older than me and hated the fact that I was so young and living it up. Her name was Donna. I'll never forget.

"So, Donna decides that she is going to come after Rome on some 'I'm pregnant' shit. Oh, this bitch had her story down pat. She called me up on the phone, at our house no less, and told me this elaborate story of how she met Rome at Platinum Plus, this strip club all the pimps and hustlers would go to. Rome was throwing a bachelor party for his right hand man, Tank. I never went out to those types of parties with him; he didn't like me around those types of crowds.

"I could tell her story was bogus because the first thing she said was that Rome was drunk. Rome never drank. He was too paranoid to let himself loose. Rome would be the only sober person in the room checking out who was coming in, and the nearest exit. The man had eyes in the back

of his head. See, someone was always trying to get Rome, and he knew this, so the last thing he would do was drink, especially in a strip club. Well, Donna hits me with 'Rome was drunk and we went back to my place and had sex.'"

"You didn't think he could have?" I interrupted.

"Hell no. I'm not saying Rome didn't cheat on me 'cause that is a possibility, and as a matter of fact, I know he did, but he wasn't gonna go to some bitch's house he just met. He would have taken her to a hotel—this was all a part of his paranoia. Well, she continues the lie with how he was going to leave me for her, and how she was just calling to give me a heads up so that I could pack my shit and move out 'cause Rome told her he was going to move her in."

"Wow, she was bold."

"Oh, it gets better. For the next nine months, she made our life a living hell. She blew up my house phone daily, busted out my car windows and even threw a brick through our living room window. She was pissed because Rome openly denied her baby, and as bad as I wanted to beat that bitch to death, I wouldn't allow myself to fight a pregnant girl. After a while, I couldn't take any more, and me and Rome separated for six months. Of course he swore up and down that he never touched the girl, but I was starting to believe her. Why else would she come at us so damn hard? She wore me down to the point where my relationship with Rome started to suffer. By the time I kicked him out, I didn't even care if the baby was his or not. I didn't want to deal with the drama anymore. He got himself an apartment on the other side of town and stayed there until after the baby was born."

"What happened when the baby was born?" Butter had my full attention.

"Well, back then DNA wasn't cracking like that, so we did a blood test. It turned out that there was an eighty percent chance that Rome was not the father. That was good enough for me. I went and found that bitch and beat the brakes off her ass. Rome moved back in and asked me to marry him. A year later we were married, and a year and a half after that he was in prison. I never got the chance to give him babies. I regret every day that I let her separate us. I wish I would have known then how precious our time together would be."

"I think about Marla's baby all the time," I admitted. "I just don't know if I can be happy with Kayne if that child is his, because I wouldn't have been able to give him his first child. She will always come first."

"No, baby, that's where you're wrong. You will always come first as long as you two are together. Don't ever let another female come between what you've built with someone you love. If you know he loves you, accept that, and be happy. Don't be like me. I know it will hurt you to know he has a child by someone else, but it will eventually go away. Let it heal, but don't bruise your relationship in the process."

"I understand what you're saying."

"As you get older you understand more and more."

Not long after, Jason and Marla walked back out of the house and pulled off. Then Chris pulled up and went inside. Minutes later, we saw a dope fiend knock on the door. She was let in by Shalauna and came out exactly one

minute later.

"Well, we know there's drugs inside," Butter said. We watched for another thirty minutes before we saw Kayne's car pull up. Shalauna and Chris got in.

"You think we should follow them?" I asked.

"No, I'll come back to scope out the place on Tuesday. Most likely, they're going to re-up. I know Shalauna always cops at the start of the week. She probably just served that lady the last of her shit. Don't worry. We'll have her ass by Wednesday."

"Sounds good to me," I said as we pulled off, headed back to my house.

Chapter 23

Tuesday—February 13, 2007

I sat inside my car with Butter watching Peachy in action. She had been a loyal snitch for over a year and owed Butter a favor. We already had her set up with another place to cop her dope so when this one went down, she'd be straight.

"What you got today?" she said to Shalauna when the door was opened. Peachy stepped inside and looked around.

"How much you got?"

"Twenty," Peachy told her.

Shalauna handed Peachy two small rocks from the inside of an Advil bottle. Peachy acted like she needed a hit, and bad. She tripped as she held her hand out to retrieve them. She fell up against Shalauna, then onto the

floor. "Clumsy bitch!" Shalauna retorted.

"I'm ... I'm sorry," Peachy said meekly, displaying her almost toothless grin as she gathered her composure and took the two rocks.

"Don't smoke it too fast," Shalauna laughed, "you might see dead bodies." She opened the door, roughly pushing Peachy out.

Shalauna had hated Peachy since their sophomore year in high school. She found out that Peachy was plotting on her man, Demontez. Not too long afterward, Peachy's plot worked, and they ended up at a fuck-by-the-hour motel. Peachy's mouth did her no good because she told everyone her plan. It got back to Shalauna, who watched from her mama's car while the two walked into room 111. Shalauna got out and walked right up to the window. She peered through the half-closed curtains and peeped her man wasting no time getting to work. Watching Demontez devour Peachy's perfect body as if it were the best thing he'd ever had, Shalauna became angry. She picked up the closest thing to her and busted into the room while Demontez was on the down stroke in Peachy's pussy. Just as he was about to pull out and nut on Peachy's titties, Shalauna clugged a brick upside his head, knocking him out cold. Unfortunately, her anger got the best of her and she hit him repeatedly. The blows were so intense, he went into convulsions while still inside of Peachy. He died from massive brain trauma.

Shalauna was so stoked, she tortured Peachy by kicking her in the head and whatever other part of her body was visible.

"Don't move now, bitch!" Shalauna yelled at Peachy every time she kicked her. She even made her stay lodged up under Demontez for at least an hour after he stopped breathing. Every part of Demontez's body was stiff, including his dick still in her.

Peachy was never the same after that. Even with the seed he accidentally deposited inside of her that night growing inside her, Peachy knew of nothing to take away the pain but drugs. Her habit resolved her pregnancy problem, but by that time, she was a full blown addict.

"Fuckin' bitch!" Peachy said, getting back into the car.

"What you see?" Butter asked anxiously.

"I can't stand her!"

"What you see?" Butter asked again.

"Shit ..." Peachy said, snapping back to reality. "Uh ... I saw a bunch of weed, but I know she got other shit because I bought some rocks. There's a lot of heat up in there, too."

"That's it?"

"I'm sure there's more."

"Was she alone?"

"Nah, she had her flunkies in there, but they'll go, too. But hey, look what I got." She smiled and held a cell phone in plain view.

"What's that?" I asked.

"It's a cell phone." Peachy looked at me like I was severely retarded.

"I know that, but whose cell phone is it?"

"Shalauna's."

"Well, I guess it's time for part two." We all smiled.

"You sure you got the right number, Peachy?"

"I may be on crack, but I ain't dumb," she snapped, then we all laughed. "Yeah, it's the right number."

I dialed the number that Peachy recited and waited for the beep. I entered my call-back number and put 911 behind it. Within minutes, the phone rang.

"What's up, shorty?" Chris yelled over music in the background.

"When you comin' through?" Butter spoke, activating the phone's speaker, disguising her voice.

"I'm wit' my nigga right now, what's up?"

"Shit, I'm tryin to see what's up wit' you. You wit' that nigga Keon?"

"Yeah, we at the club."

"Well, when y'all finish, roll through here. I got some dime pieces here that wanna do the damn thing."

"Straight up! How many?"

"Don't matter, just bring some of yo' boys." Butter heard a hand muffle the phone, then Chris came back. "A'ight, bet. We'll be over later."

I instantly caught an attitude. I knew Chris would be up for it, but the fact that Kayne was with him pissed me off even more. Butter read my mind. "Kayne ain't doin' nothin', girl. That man loves you."

"Yeah, but I heard him in the background talking." I was seething. "Out there in the club kickin' it while we out here on a fuckin' stakeout with no food!"

Everybody laughed.

We all stayed inside of the car, waiting to see what we could see. Four hours later, at four thirty-six a.m., we

were startled by Shalauna's cell phone ringing. We looked at the Caller ID, and it was the number we had called earlier. Butter answered, and Chris told her that they were on their way. He also informed her that he had a business associate from out of town with him and asked if he'd be able to be accommodated as well. Butter assured him that anything would go, which was true. Everything was fair game tonight.

After Butter hung up, she called the local precinct.

"Hi, this is Officer Morris. May I help you?"

"I'm so sick and tired of these drug dealers!" Butter spoke properly, but with a southern twang.

"Ma'am, what are you talking about?"

"I can't even come home without these ... these black ... whatdayouwannacallit," she emphasized the word 'black,' "men offering me some of that ... that ... crank!"

"Ma'am, do you mean crack?"

"Crank, crack, same thing. I'm just afraid to come home at night."

"Ma'am, where do you live?"

"I live at 5620 Fredrick Avenue. There's a run down house in front of me. I see ungodly people going in and out of there at all times of the day, but it's mostly early morning, around four thirty or so."

"Ma'am, if I can have the address where you see the suspicious activity, I'll send some officers out that way."

Butter gave them Shalauna's address and was promised that officers would be dispatched immediately.

"This has to work," we all said as I started my car and drove off. Before we could get on the main street, we saw

Chris' truck turn the corner. He'd taken the bait. I dropped Butter and Peachy off and headed home. I prayed that Kayne wasn't with them.

"Lord, please don't let anything happen to him."

Chapter 24

Wednesday—February 14, 2007

The set up against Shalauna, Chris and Derrick went perfectly, with no trace of me and Kayne being the master minds behind it all. I turned on the morning news and there it was: "And for today's top story, due to an anonymous tip, a very profitable drug ring in the city has been disbanded—"

"Kayne? Kayne!" I yelled excitedly. I didn't even listen to the rest of the report. "Kayne?!" He didn't answer. I walked swiftly through the condo. No Kayne. Immediately, I began panicking. "Kayne wasn't here the last time this shit went down. No! It can't be happening again!" I said to myself as I paced the floor.

The vibration of my cell phone scared me. I looked at the Caller ID, and my heart started beating rapidly.

"Hello?" I said, out of breath.

"Hey, baby."

"Where are you?" I asked with worry in my voice.

"I'm at the police station—"

"Police station. Kayne …" I cried uncontrollably. "Not again, baby, I can't go through this again."

"Mina, listen to me."

He paused.

I cried.

"Mina!"

"Yes," I sniffled.

"I'm fine, baby. The police called me because there was some type of drug raid." Kayne spoke as if he knew nothing, just in case someone else was listening. "Isaiah was in the house when they raided, so now they're investigating Marla."

"You're kidding me!"

"No, I'm not. They gave me temporary custody, so …"

"Are you serious? It's Valentine's Day! I thought we were going to be alone." I was being insensitive to the fact that the baby was involved, but I didn't care.

"Baby, just go along with it," Kayne pleaded. "I'm going to call and schedule a test for tomorrow after I get him to the house."

"Yeah, you do that," I said, hanging up. I couldn't believe he had the nerve to sign a birth certificate for that baby.

I finished the work day without even bothering to look for Marla. I knew she was already gone. As I got off the elevator and walked toward my front door, I could hear the baby screaming from the hallway on my way in the house. I rolled my eyes, dreading having to deal with another bitch's brat for who knew how long. Kayne sensed my mood when I came in and tried everything in his power to quiet the baby down, but nothing worked. I took the baby out of his arms and walked around the room rocking him, not because I cared, but because I wanted him to shut up. Marla called Kayne and he spoke to her in private while I tended to Isaiah.

"What did she say?" I asked, seeing that Isaiah had fallen asleep.

"Nothing, she's happy I got him. She's been wanting me to spend more time with him." I rolled my eyes and went to the bedroom to lay him down. Kayne followed behind me.

"Now that he's asleep, we can start our Valentine's Day. I'm going to cook for you, baby." He pulled me close, but I was beyond pissed.

"Did you make the appointment?"

"Yeah, it's tomorrow morning at ten. You off, right?"

"Yes. What did they find?"

"A brick, a carbon fifteen, a .357, a twelve gauge and three pounds of weed."

"Good, I'm going to sleep." I slipped my clothes off and put on a T-shirt. Lying in the bed next to Marla's baby, I fell asleep for the rest of the night. I woke up the next morning to an empty bed. I went to the living room, where I found Kayne already dressed and changing Isaiah's diaper.

"It's nine fifteen, baby. You better get ready so we won't be late." Saying nothing, I took a five minute shower and threw on a comfortable velour jogging suit.

After they were tested, Kayne was told the results would be ready February 28th, two days after we returned from California. Marla made arrangements for Kayne to take Isaiah to her sister's before we left on the 23rd . She was so happy about Isaiah being with Kayne that she didn't even bother to investigate where her baby was living for the week. She even tried to get him to take Isaiah with him to visit his family in California, but of course, that was not about to happen.

* * * *

After a week of being with her baby, who cried more than he slept, I was so happy to escape to California. When we touched down, Kayne's cousin Quinn was at the airport to pick us up. He was handsome just like Kayne and appeared to be in his mid-thirties. There was already a family affair going on in celebration of Kayne coming home when we arrived at his mother's house. Her house was a classic California-style home made of white stone with shingles at the top. It was a gorgeous three bedroom ranch with a brand new built-in patio. She had a beautiful lagoon-shaped pool with lights and lounge chairs surrounding it that looked beautiful at night.

She welcomed me as if she had known me forever and was honestly one of the most beautiful women I had ever seen. Her skin looked as if it were made of caramel, and her silky hair hung to the middle of her back. Her shape was more distinct than an hour glass. I also met his only aunt, Rita, who resembled his mother, and her sons, Cory and Dante, who would both be groomsmen in the wedding. I even got to meet India who was even cuter in person and so excited about being the flower girl. After partying with a house full of people, I was exhausted. I went to bed and woke up to a wonderful breakfast that Carla, Kayne's mother, fixed especially for me and Kayne.

As we discussed the plans for the wedding, Carla came up with all kinds of decorative ideas. She definitely had an eye for style, so I agreed to let her be in charge of the whole reception. As we talked and became more familiar with each other, she began to go into Kayne's childhood, eventually pulling out all kinds of old pictures of him. He had to literally pull us away from the kitchen table to get ready to go see the beach and the properties. I was so excited that I was dressed in nearly fifteen minutes.

The beach was absolutely perfect for the wedding; I especially loved the big rock that sat on the shore. The beach was just big enough to set up a nice-sized tent for the reception. Next, we went to look at the house Kayne had bought. It needed a lot of work, but it definitely had potential. Both condos were on the same street, Sunup, at the bend of the cul-de-sac. The other two-bedroom reminded me a lot of my place back in Cincinnati. I was sure he would be getting a nice piece of change for it once he rented it out. But the two-bedroom we would be living in was to die for. It was equipped with vaulted ceilings, two full bathrooms, a patio in back, a balcony connected to the master bedroom and a huge cherry-wood decorated kitchen with an island in the middle.

When we finally got home from the overwhelming day,

Kayne went out for drinks with Quinn while Carla and I relaxed poolside. She began telling me the story of her abusive boyfriend, who Kayne murdered. I told her my mother's story and she related. She was happy to hear that Markus was behind bars, but what shocked me the most was when she told me that she knew Kayne was the one who killed her boyfriend.

"I've always felt like a horrible mother for putting my son in a position where he might have to spend the rest of his life behind bars. It was a miracle he wasn't caught," she said, shaking her head. "But I love Keon more than the life inside my body. I never told him that I knew because I didn't want him to feel any remorse for what he did. He didn't hurt me, he saved me.

"Raising a boy on these mean streets is tough, and I always had to have something to fall back on, just in case he got into some type of trouble. And as we know, trouble can find anyone, regardless if they're looking for it or not." I nodded my head in agreement. "Ever since I moved from Chicago, I've been putting money away for him. We used some of it when he had his case, but there's still more where that came from. That'll be my gift to you all on your wedding day. A trust fund for your children." She smiled proudly.

"That's beautiful, Carla. I know he will be so thankful for it. You know, I've seen so many people grow up without ever having anything or anyone to care about them past the age of seventeen. I'm truly grateful for you, my mother and my father. I am so blessed to have people who care for me. It took me a while to realize it, but I know now that I'm older that everyone isn't as lucky to be surrounded by love. I'm so happy to be a part of your family. You all have made me feel so welcome." I leaned over to hug her.

"I'm happy to have you in the family, sweetheart. It will be like having the daughter I've always wanted." She hugged me back. "Now remember, this has to stay between us until the wedding day."

"Of course." I smiled.

* * * *

On Sunday we went to church with Carla and Rita before catching our three o'clock flight. As soon as we got back into the city, Marla was calling Kayne's phone to see if he was home and to tell him Isaiah needed to stay with him because her sister had to work. I was instantly irritated when I realized he was on the phone with her. I hated hearing them talk. He was always too nice for my liking, and it seemed like I could always hear her voice through the phone. He picked the baby up from Marla's sister that night, and before he even brought him home, I decided he was on his own with Isaiah, because I really didn't feel like being bothered. I completely ignored Kayne and the baby, making them sleep in the living room Sunday and Monday night. I guess he understood how hurt I was feeling, so he didn't argue with me about sleeping alone. He didn't know, but I really appreciated that.

Chapter 25

Wednesday—February 28, 2007

Kayne begged me to go with him to pick up the results of the paternity test. On my lunch break, I met him at the testing center. As we walked in together, I felt myself becoming a little nauseous just thinking about what the results could be. I wanted Marla out of the picture once and for all. As I was thinking of all the drama that would arise once she finally found out who I was, I was suddenly face to face with her. She was sitting with a case worker in the waiting room, going over paperwork. There was nowhere to run or hide.

Her face beamed as she saw Kayne walking with the baby, but her smile quickly faded when her eyes caught mine, a few steps behind.

"Mya, what are you doing here?" She brushed past

Kayne. I could tell she really didn't get it. She was now standing between us, looking back and forth trying to put the pieces together. "Keon, what the fuck is going on? Mya, I just saw you at work. Did you follow me here? Did you two come together?" she shouted, standing only inches from me.

"Her name is Amina, and she's here with me." Kayne made sure not to raise his voice. Isaiah was sleeping in his arms and the social worker was staring dead at us.

"What the fuck are you doing here with my fiancé?" She looked at me with contempt in her eyes.

"You mean *my* fiancé." I waved my engagement ring in her face. She raised her hand to slap me in the face, but I caught it and twisted her whole arm around. "Bitch, don't make me hurt you," I growled in her ear.

With a terrified look in her eyes, she backed away. Tears built up as she tried to swing on Kayne with full force. He backed away, trying to keep the baby from getting hit. "Yo, you need to chill. I'm just here to get the results of this test!" Kayne yelled angrily as security came to restrain Marla.

"You been fucking the bitch I work with!" she yelled at Kayne, then turned to me. "And you was supposed to be my friend!" she shouted, looking at me with murder in her eyes. "Give me my fucking baby you lying piece of shit!" She struggled against the guards.

"Just go get the results. I'll keep him out here," the case worker told Kayne, taking Isaiah, who was screaming louder than his mother.

We waited in the reception area for ten minutes until

Kayne's name was called. The whole time I could hear Marla going on and on to the case worker about how she couldn't wait to see the look on our faces when the results revealed that Kayne was the father. She also said something about child support and taking us for everything we had.

"Mr. Keon NaCore," the lady at the front desk called. Marla and Kayne walked back to the doctor's office.

"Don't let that bitch next to *our* son," Marla instructed the case worker as she stood up to enter the office, watching me the whole time.

While they were gone, I couldn't help but stare at that little boy. A big part of me felt so sorry for him. He shouldn't have been in this mess and honestly, being pregnant was making me especially sensitive to the matter. I looked around the waiting room at the five or so women who were there with their kids, some as old as ten or twelve and the men they were testing as potential fathers. This place was full of sadness. I remembered how I had felt all those years thinking that my father didn't care about me, how he'd left me and my moms struggling. But I was lucky. He wanted me, and he found me. Granted I was already well into my teens, but getting that letter from him asking to meet me made me feel whole.

That is what I wanted for Marla's son. I wanted him to grow up knowing that Jason or, God forbid, Kayne, was his dad. No ifs, ands or buts about it. If he turned out to be Kayne's, I would have to accept it. I wouldn't treat him any differently than I would treat my own.

Isaiah was a big six months, and as he sat in the case

worker's lap he smiled and babbled and looked at me, not knowing that I was the woman who ruined his mother's life. I looked in his eyes and couldn't tell, as much as I tried, if Kayne was his father or not. I bit my lip in anticipation of what was to come. I thought about calling Kelly for comfort, but there was too much I would have to explain, and I didn't want to be stuck on the phone when Kayne came walking through the doors. The fifteen minutes I had been waiting felt like hours.

Finally, Kayne busted through the doors, yelling and screaming with the results in his hand.

"Yeah, that's what I'm talking about!" yelled Kayne. "Mina, baby, let's get the fuck outta here." I snatched the papers from his hand to read them for myself.

"Where is Marla?" asked the case worker.

"In the back crying her eyes out," said Kayne. "You better get back there. I think she gonna try and kill herself over this."

With the help of a nurse, Marla came sobbing into the waiting room, making even more of a scene.

"Yeah, bitch, take this bullshit to Maury 'cause you obviously don't know who the father of that little bastard is." I threw the results in her face.

"This shit ain't over, you backstabbing bitch!" she hissed, grabbing Isaiah from the case worker.

"Marla, it's over. Amina is the only girl I want. We're getting married, and I don't want shit to do with your lying, cheating ass," Kayne said, pulling me away. "Let's go. Don't say shit else!" he yelled at me when I tried to lunge back toward her.

"This is the same bitch that left you cold? You told me your name was Mya!"

"No, sweetie, I'm Amina, the one who had Kayne before you. And get this right." I pulled away from Kayne and walked back to Marla. "I never left him. Kayne and I had and still have a love you will never know. I went to jail for him because I'm not a snitch like your cousin, Shalauna. I kept it tight for him because I'm not a slut like you. More importantly, I know who the father of my child is," I said, patting my stomach.

"Keon, how could you let her do this to us?" she cried. Kayne held my arm and led me out to the parking lot.

"You need to go home," he said as he closed my car door.

"I have to go back to work."

"No, I said go home. Call them and tell them you quit."

"What the fuck is your problem? You act like you're not even happy to be rid of that bitch!"

"I am, but I want you to quit before things get worse. I don't want you dealing with her at work. Amina, go home. You have our baby to take care of and a wedding to plan. You don't need that job!" He walked away angrily to his car.

I put my car in drive and did as I was told. He was right. I didn't need that job. I deserved to lay around the house all day, feed myself and the baby and prepare for my wedding. I also needed time to look into moving to California and enrolling in school. I had already spoken to my parole officer, and she told me everything would be transferred by July 5th which meant I had to be a resident of California by then. Things were going as planned for once. I just hoped I wasn't getting too used to it.

Chapter 26

Saturday—March 3, 2007

It was Butter's 75th day clean. Kelly and I decided to take her to the restaurant of her choice to celebrate.

"Let's go to Outback. I want a big-ass steak!" Butter said excitedly when I called her.

"Outback it is," I confirmed as Kelly and I hit the highway, headed to Butter's new one bedroom apartment where she now stayed, alone and far away from the city. With a new attitude and new surroundings, it seemed as if nothing could stop her. I only hoped nothing would stand in her way on her road to recovery.

"So how does it feel, Butter?" Kelly asked as they sat sipping martinis while I drank a sparkling water.

"Girl, I truly feel like a whole new person. I never want to go back to that life, and God willing, I never will. My

husband is so proud of me. I could never disappoint him again."

"Words cannot express how proud I am of you," I told her.

"Yeah, me too. I'm so happy to see you back on top, girl," Kelly added.

"Thank you, ladies, and allow me to reintroduce myself to you both. I am Andrea Malone, and I am an ex-addict."

"It's nice to meet you, Andrea. I guess we have to say goodbye to Butter now."

"No, just make sure you don't put Butter on the program for the wedding!" We all fell out laughing.

"Did Mina tell you about the results of the paternity test with Marla's baby?" Kelly asked Butter.

"No, I forgot all about it. What did it say, girl?"

"You are NOT the father!" I said, imitating the talk show host Maury Povich, known best for paternity testing.

"Oh my goodness, are you serious? So whose baby is it? The gay dude?"

"What gay dude?" Kelly questioned.

I couldn't help laughing at Butter's bluntness.

"The dude who was with Marla. I don't remember his name, but I know he's gay. I saw him more than a few times downtown with that drag queen named Wave. You know she be down on Vine selling ass every night. I should have said something a long time ago." I nearly choked on my steak. I instantly thought of Marla telling me she wanted an HIV test. I had somehow blocked the whole thing out of my mind. I was so obsessed with revenge that I had somehow forgotten about this terrible threat.

"What! Are you serious? Amina, you never told me he was gay!" Kelly was beyond shocked.

"Marla told me in December that he was bisexual and that she needed to get an HIV test. Oh my God, what if I got it? What if Kayne does—"

"Baby, calm down," Butter interrupted. "Everything is going to be fine." She came over to my side of the booth to comfort me.

"Amina, you can call and make an appointment for a test first thing Monday morning," Kelly said, grabbing my hand from across the table.

"I can't wait that long. I need to go to the hospital. What if I have it? My baby will get it. I don't want to lose my baby." I began crying as I revealed the secret I had been keeping for over two months.

"Baby?" Butter and Kelly both said in unison with huge grins on their faces.

"Yeah, I wanted it to be a surprise." I was extremely disappointed that the cat was out of the bag.

"I knew something was up when you didn't order a martini," Kelly said, taking a peek at my stomach.

"Sweetie, that's a wonderful thing. I'm sure God will not let your joy be ruined by anything," Butter said, hugging me tightly.

"That's right, Amina. That baby inside of you is a blessing that will keep you safe from any harm." Kelly moved my bangs from my eyes.

"I'm sorry I ruined your celebration dinner, Butter," I said, drying my eyes.

"Girl, you know you ain't ruined nothing. Now go in the

bathroom and clean yourself up so we can discuss the engagement party me and Kelly want to throw you." She smiled and got up to let me out.

I went to the restroom and pulled myself together enough to finish the rest of the night pleasantly, but the thought that my life could be in danger weighed heavily on my mind. After dropping Butter off, Kelly took me home.

"Girl, you know what you need to do. Just get the test to be safe, even though I know everything will be fine. I'm praying for you and your baby." She hugged me tightly before I got out of the car. As I came inside to an empty house, closing the door behind me, I noticed an envelope on the floor that someone had slid under the door. The envelope was blank. I opened it, pulling out a card with the words "Congratulations on Your Wedding" on the front. When I read the words inside, my heart stopped.

Amina and Keon,

Congratulations on your engagement. I hope you all find happiness in each other forever more.

Hopefully the HIV virus I have contracted will not affect you, your happy home and your new baby.

Best wishes,

Marla.

I dialed her number in a flash, and she answered on the second ring.

"Bitch, what kind of sick joke you trying to play!" I screamed into the phone, feeling like I was losing myself all over again.

"It's no joke. Go find out for yourself." She hung up, and I fell to the floor in overwhelming despair. Feeling sharp pains shooting through my stomach, I grabbed the card and hit the door for the emergency room.

After waiting an hour, I was finally inside an examination room. The doctor conducted a sonogram and concluded that nothing was wrong with the baby. I had phoned Kayne and told him everything. I could tell by his voice that he was shook, but he would never let me know it. After I showed the doctor the card from Marla, they tested me for HIV and advised me to press harassment charges, which I had already made up my mind to do. My results would be ready in two weeks. Kayne told me he would go to the clinic Monday and be tested, too. As soon as I walked through the door, he pulled me into his arms. I tried my best to hold it together, but I was scared.

"Is the baby okay?" he asked still holding me.

"Yes."

"Everything is going to be okay, baby. I promise." I knew he was only trying to comfort me. I could feel his heart beating fast.

"What if it's not?" I looked at him with a tear-streaked face.

"Have I ever made a promise I didn't keep?" I searched for worry in his eyes, but to my surprise I found sureness.

"Baby, I felt like I was going to lose it again when I read that card. I thought I was going to lose my mind. I don't want to go back there."

"And you never will. Now come on and let me give you

a bath." He led me into the bedroom where he completely undressed me, then ran a hot bubble bath. He started with my hair and worked his way down. When he was done he laid me down on the bed and gave me a full body massage with hot oil. By the time he was done, I was crossing over into a deep sleep that I didn't want to wake up from.

Chapter 27

Monday—March 19, 2007

I walked out of the clinic feeling as if a thousand pounds had been lifted off my heart. Both Kayne and I tested negative for HIV. I wasn't only concerned about the whole Marla, Jason and Kayne sex triangle, but the fact I had slept with Chris without a condom. The thought of getting something from that dirty snake or even worse, passing something on to Kayne or our child, was what really had me sitting on pins and needles for days.

You would think that I would have been on top of the world having gotten my man back, being pregnant and engaged. Instead, I shut down. I locked myself in my room and fell into a depression. All of the careless acts I had committed throughout the years had finally caught up to me. Even the ones that were forced upon me could have held serious and deadly consequences. Kayne treated me like a queen and respected my need for privacy. I wanted for nothing during this time.

A few days later, after leaving my room for my daily shower, Kayne suggested lunch. I noticed the clear skies and sun shining brightly, so I agreed. That was just what I needed to get me out of my depression.

It was good to be outside, and the only thing on my mind was planning my wedding. I had neglected it for months. The only thing we had set in stone was that it was going to be in Cali on the beach. I invited Kelly and Butter over to help me flip through the dozen bridal and fashion magazines I bought on my way back to the house. By the time they got to the house, I had converted the living room into a bridal boutique. The mission for the day was to finalize the details. By four o'clock we had picked a dress for them to wear, and Kayne had told us what he wanted the groomsmen to wear. He even insisted on having them wear gators even after I told him we were going to be standing on a beach in July. Their feet were going to get fried, I joked.

As we looked through dozens of bridal magazines trying to decide on what type of dress I wanted to wear, I decided that whatever dress I chose, I was going to wait until June to be fitted. Any dress I fell in love with now was surely not going to fit me in three months.

With the bulk of the work done, the girls and I watched our favorite movie, "*Poetic Justice*." Kayne came back from grabbing us some Buffalo Wild Wings, greeting the three of us with a smile. He was really happy to see me back to

myself. As we dug into the food, my cell phone rang.

"Hello?" I answered without looking at the number.

"How are the wedding plans coming along?" Marla asked with a laugh.

"Better than yours." My tone of voice caused everyone to stop eating and listen in.

"Is that Marla?" Kelly mouthed. I nodded my head yes. She took the phone from my hands while Marla was talking and put the phone on speaker.

"I guess catching the bug didn't stop you two," Marla continued. "Must really be love." I wanted to jump through the phone and kill her nasty ass.

"Bitch, I don't have shit and neither does Kayne."

"Marla, stop playing games, man," Kayne jumped in.

"Keon!" Marla gasped.

"You stopped being a part of our lives when the test came back and little man wasn't mine."

"Keon, baby, you need to come home." All of her gangsta turned to tears once she heard his voice. "I never meant to hurt you. Please, we need you here."

"Marla, give it a rest."

"Mya, you stay the fuck out of this."

"It's Mina, bitch." Kayne grabbed my arm to let me know to fall back.

"Marla, we have nothing else to say to you. If you call again we're going to have real problems." He pressed the speaker button to end the call then pulled me close to him.

"You want me to go over there and fuck her up?" Butter asked after a moment of silence.

"Nah, save your energy. She's not worth it," I told her.

"She sounds crazy," Kelly chimed in. "You guys need to file a police report. From the sound of her voice, I don't think she's gonna stop."

"You're right," agreed Kayne. "I've never heard her sound like this. Baby, first thing in the morning, you're going to the precinct. I don't fuck with the police, but this shit gotta stop. Kelly, can you go with her?"

"Of course."

"I'll be back." He grabbed his keys off the counter, took a chicken wing and left.

As soon as the door closed behind him, Butter started. "I wasn't going to say anything before because I thought we were done with her." She sat on the edge of the couch with her plate in her lap. Kelly and my eyes were glued to her. "I heard she's shooting dog now."

"What!" Kelly was shocked, but I couldn't care less.

"Yep. I ran into an old smoking buddy of mine downtown, and he told me that these days, Shalauna's house is the new den. From what he's seen, Marla is spending most of her days there now. She's even taken to turning tricks. He told me he and four other dope fiends fucked her in the basement of Shalauna's crib. I told him I hoped he used a condom."

"Why is she crashing at Shalauna's?" I couldn't believe she was turned out that hard.

"He told me that she's been staying there since she lost her job."

"What, she lost her job?" Kelly asked.

"And the baby," Butter added. "Child Services came and took the baby once they found out that Shalauna had been

watching him while Marla worked. You know the state already had an open case on her. They took her three kids away from her almost a year ago."

"For what?" I asked. Learning about Marla's family history really shined a light on her antics.

"Shalauna's oldest boy took some crack he found in her refrigerator to school. She lied and said she didn't know where he found it, but they didn't believe her. That, and the kids always came to school dirty and with bruises. Rumor has it that one of her own customers called her in over Marla's son. Guess they saw her doing some foul shit to the baby. Marla's mother is trying to get him back."

"Damn, sounds like she lost everything," Kelly said, shaking her head.

"Yeah, everything including her mind. If she ever calls me again, I swear I'll track that dope fiend bitch down and kill her."

"Girl, don't worry about her, you're on your way out of this city anyway. However, you definitely need to press harassment charges if she keeps this up."

"I ain't playing with that girl. She's been calling Kayne's phone, too, and we're both fed up. I won't change my number just because that crazy bitch can't accept that she fucked her own life up and lost something good."

"True," Kelly said in agreement.

* * * *

The next morning, Kelly came by the house and picked me up to go to the precinct. Butter had spent the night with

me, so she came along for the ride. Marla had definitely pushed me over the edge because I never thought I'd see the day I'd voluntarily walk into a police department. As I entered the doors, a knot settled in my throat.

"May I help you?" asked the officer behind the front desk.

"Yes, I'd like to file a police report against someone."

"For what?" He seemed to find my request slightly humorous.

"Harassment."

"Let me guess. It's a woman."

"Yes, how'd you know?"

"What's her name?" He pulled out a form from under the counter.

"Marla ... Marla ... Damn, I can't remember her last name."

"Well, take this. Fill out what you do know and bring it back to me."

As I walked over to an empty chair my mind was completely blank. I'd heard of mommy brain, but this was horrible. I pulled out my cell. "Kayne, what's Marla's last name?"

"Johnson. Where you at?"

"You know where I am. I'll talk to you later."

I filled out her name and other info, then walked back up to the counter. I felt so weird being in there, like a snitch. Fuck it, she deserved it. "Here you go." I slid the form to the officer.

"What exactly did she do to you?" He pulled out a pen to make a note on the form.

"She endangered my life."

"How?" He looked up from the desk, anticipating my answer.

"By spreading HIV. She threatened to infect me and my unborn child any way she could. Last night I found a needle in my mailbox. If I didn't look inside I would have stuck my finger right on it." I had to build it up because I knew the cops weren't going to take her annoying phone calls as a threat.

"Well, ma'am, we will definitely look into it and bring her in for questioning."

"Thank you." I turned around and walked out the door.

Chapter 28

Sunday—May 6, 2007

It was my baby's twenty-sixth birthday. I had plans to take Kayne to dinner later in the evening and to a comedy show at The Funny Bone to see Katt Williams, the comedian from Cincinnati. I knew Kayne would be thrilled because he had missed the last show because we were in California. First thing that morning, I woke him up with a small ice cream cake with a lit candle in the middle, topped off with a happy birthday song.

"Happy birthday to you. Happy birthday to you. Happy birthday, dear baby, happy birthday to you!" I sang before watching him blow out the candle.

"Thank you, baby," he grinned, giving me a kiss.

I cooked breakfast—waffles, eggs, bacon, sausage and a fruit salad I made with cantaloupe, watermelon, grapes and

peaches. "Come on, baby, let's eat," I said, leading him to the table I had laid out buffet style. "After we eat, then we can cut the cake."

"This looks good, smells good, too," Kayne said, admiring everything.

"Do you have plans for tonight?" I asked. "If not, I want to take you out."

"Of course not. My plan is whatever you have planned for me." He smiled, grabbing a few slices of bacon.

"Okay, sounds good. We're leaving at six thirty, so be ready and looking your best." I winked.

"Where we going?" he asked with a big grin on his face.

"To eat, where did you think?" I said, not wanting to give my surprise away. "Isn't that what pregnant women do all the time?" We both laughed.

"But, baby, it's my birthday," Kayne said, rubbing my stomach.

We sat down and began eating. "Well, since you put it that way," I joked, "how about going to the Montgomery Inn?"

"We need reservations for that, baby," Kayne said between bites of food. I looked at him and raised an eyebrow. "Okay, baby, the Montgomery Inn." He knew something was up. "Do I need to make a trip to Wendel's?" he asked, referring to one of the best clothing stores in the city.

"Boy, you got plenty of clothes in the closet that still got the tags on them," I laughed. "But if you want to go to Wendel's, you can pick something. After all, it is your birthday," I joked.

"Cool! You know how I got to step out."

"Oh yeah, baby, I know. I think I might pick me up something, too."

After breakfast, cake and some bed and shower sex, we went downtown to cop some brand new outfits for the night. Kayne had his clothes picked out within ten minutes. I, on the other hand, took an hour to figure out what would set me ahead of everybody else who would be in the spot. When we got home, I was exhausted—all a part of being pregnant. Kayne and I took a nap together, waking up at five thirty to get ready to leave. By six forty-five, we were headed to the boathouse at the Montgomery Inn.

We spent an hour and a half enjoying each other's company, talking about our future and trying out baby names. Afterward, we headed to the car. I was stuffed.

"Put your seatbelt on, baby," Kayne reminded me as soon as we got in the car. I did as I was told, loosening the strap that was tightly hugging my belly.

As I carefully backed out of my parking space, a car came speeding toward me. *Bam!* The impact hit my side of the car. I jerked forward, hitting my head on the steering wheel.

"Baby, you okay?!" Kayne panicked, putting the car in park for me.

I only nodded my head. I felt dizzy, so I stayed put as Kayne quickly jumped out of the car.

"What the fuck is yo' problem?" he yelled, approaching the all-white Nissan Maxima with tinted windows and dented sides. Whoever was driving the hooptie sat in the car and watched him yell. "You ain't see us backing up, muthafucka! Get the fuck out the damn car!"

By now, people who were walking into the restaurant had noticed the scene.

"Sir, I saw what just happened," a white man who was standing near his car confirmed. "I'm going to call the police." He dialed 911 on his cell and walked back toward the restaurant, obviously not wanting to be directly in the middle of the drama. I got out of the car, although I felt safer inside. I was pissed at whoever deliberately rammed their car into mine.

"Stay in the car, Amina!" Kayne yelled.

"No, I want to see who in the fuck is trying to kill us!" I yelled, approaching the busted Maxima.

Kayne grabbed me by the arm. "Baby, I said get back in the car. I'll handle this," he said forcefully, looking me directly in the eye.

"I'll stand right here, but I ain't getting back in the car," I told him with my arms folded.

He huffed and walked away. Just then, Marla stepped out of the Maxima with a bat.

"Muthafucka, let that bitch bring her ass over here if she want to!" she yelled, holding the bat in the air. "I'll beat the fucking brakes off that bitch!"

"Bitch, you can put that bat down and fight me," I said, lunging toward her. Kayne caught me in his arms, holding me back. "Put the bat down, bitch! Put it down! Let's go ... I been ready for yo' ass for a minute!" I screamed, fighting for release.

"Baby, stop it! You ain't fighting her." Kayne held me tighter. "You pregnant, calm down." He then looked at

Marla. "Back the fuck up, man. Back up!" I still fought against Kayne's grip.

"I'll beat that baby out this bitch," Marla threatened, dropping the bat and running toward me. She started swinging and ended up hitting Kayne in the jaw. He finally let me go and pushed her back.

"Get in the car, Amina!" he warned me. Marla lunged toward me, but Kayne caught her and dragged her back to her car, kicking and screaming.

I ran to pick up the bat. "Bitch wanna come after me with a bat," I said, huffing and stomping toward her car. "Fuck that bullshit!" The next sound everyone heard was glass shattering. I bashed out Marla's headlights. "This is for fucking up my car, you dumb bitch!" The bat came down again, on the hood of the car, causing another dent.

"Amina, stop! You tryin' to get locked up again?" Kayne screamed at me. I had never seen him so mad, and I was sure he hadn't seen me this mad either. "Marla," he said. "When I let you go, you better get your crazy ass in this fucking car, or I'ma let her loose on you. Straight up!"

"Nigga, you think you just gon' leave me after we was supposed to be married!"

"Look, bitch, you ruined that shit. Now just leave me the fuck alone!"

"Fuck you, Keon!"

"Naw, fuck you. It wasn't meant to be, and you showed me that by fuckin' wit' dude."

"I loved you! You know that! I just made a mistake!" Marla said through tears.

"Kayne, let's go before I come over there and kill that

simple bitch," I spat angrily.

"Shut the fuck up! I'm talking to him," Marla yelled at me. "Stay out of it!"

"Ain't a damn thing to talk about. He don't want you. What don't you understand?"

Kayne opened the door and forced her inside. There were police sirens in the distance.

As Marla started up the car, she yelled, "You won't be having that baby!" She then floored the car, aiming for me. Kayne pushed me out of the way just in time, causing me to drop the bat. Running over it, she reversed the car again, this time bashing into the front of the patrol car that had just pulled up. Two officers got out of the car with guns drawn.

"Get out of the vehicle with your hands up!" one female officer yelled. Marla slowly stepped out of the car with her hands above her head, tears in her eyes. They rushed toward her, cuffing her and reading her her rights. After Marla was in the police car, sobbing her eyes out, I informed the police that I had already reported Marla for harassment. They told me I had three days to press charges, and there was no doubt I would.

It was now dark outside, and I looked at my watch. We still had thirty minutes to make it to the comedy show. Even though I had a headache and there was a big-ass dent in the side of my truck, I wasn't about to let this crazy bitch ruin the night I had planned for Kayne's birthday.

"Kayne, let's go. I have a surprise for you."

"Baby, you sure you don't want to go to the hospital to just make sure everything is okay?"

"I feel fine, Kayne. Are you okay?" I asked, rubbing the side of his face.

"Yeah, I'm cool."

"Good. We can deal with that bitch later, but it's your night, and I'm taking you to see Katt Williams, so let's go." I walked toward my truck. "You drive."

I got into the passenger's side and buckled my seatbelt. Kayne only smiled and drove off. When we got there, the place was packed. I wanted a drink to calm my nerves, but as soon as the show started, I was so caught up in laughter that I almost forgot what had me upset in the first place. By the end of the night, my sides were hurting from laughing so hard, and the only thing I could think about was sleep.

Back home, Kayne kissed my neck as he helped me undress. "Thanks for the great birthday, baby."

"You're welcome." I kissed him.

"I'm sorry about Marla." Kayne looked me in the eyes. "I'm so sorry, but it'll be over soon … I promise."

"I hope so," I said. I wanted to believe the words, but they sounded too good to be true.

Chapter 29

Saturday—May 26, 2007

It was a surprise. Or at least that was what Butter and Kelly thought, but I got them good. I woke up and headed straight to the hair salon where I got my hair done as well as a manicure and pedicure. Then I stopped by the mall and bought a cute peach-colored maternity tube dress from Pea in a Pod. By the time I got to the parking lot, Kayne was blowing my phone up.

"Hello, Kayne."

"Mina, where are you?"

"I'm on my way home. You want me to bring you home some IHOP?"

"No, actually I was thinking we could go out for brunch." Kayne didn't know nothing about no brunch. I knew this was the set up Butter and Kelly told him to use.

"How long before you get home?"

"About fifteen minutes."

"Well, hurry up, baby. I'm hungry."

"Okay, I'll see you shortly."

When I walked in the door, Kayne couldn't help but crack up. It wasn't even noon, and here I had been up and out since eight and came back in looking like a movie star.

"And where do you think you're going?" he asked from the living room couch.

"Negro, you know damn well where *we* are going. Now let's get ready." I pulled my new dress out of the bag. "Make sure whatever you wear today matches this."

Kayne doubled over in laughter. "Whatever you say."

* * * *

The engagement party that Kelly and Butter had put together was beautiful. It was at a Covington restaurant located on the river called The Bank. The party itself took place outside on the deck, which was reserved and set up with twelve white tables decorated with white roses. The attire was all white and everyone looked wonderful.

There were around forty people there, including all of my family, a few of my mother's friends who hadn't seen me in years, some of my grandmother's friends, my aunt Angie and Trina, who brought her mother and two little sisters. Kelly's mother also came along with two of her cousins, who were three years younger than us. Shayna and Damen were there with my baby sister, Adrianna, who was a month old. She was so precious I felt like holding her the whole

time, but there were so many people to mingle with.

"Remind me to never throw you a surprise anything ever again," Kelly joked as she rubbed my belly.

"Why?"

"Mina, don't play that with me. You come walking in here looking like a million bucks. I know you knew about this."

"Well, to be honest, I knew it was today, but if it makes you feel any better I didn't know where it was going to be." I smiled.

"Whatever. Well, I hope you like everything," Butter added.

"Of course. Thank you, ladies." I hugged the both of them then decided to make my rounds. After thanking everyone for coming I was starting to get tired and hungry. Right on cue Kelly took the microphone from the DJ.

"Hello, everyone." The crowd hushed. "I'm one of your hostesses, Kelly. I'm also the Maid of Honor. We would like for you to take a seat so that the meal can be served."

Before being served a delicious meal of grilled salmon, rice pilaf and asparagus followed by New York style cheesecake, everyone joined in on a toast to our happiness. After eating, I decided it was the perfect time to let the rest of my family and friends in on my pregnancy. I was six months pregnant and showing, but the dress I had on was still concealing my bump. I stood, asking for everyone's attention.

"I would like to first of all thank each one of you for coming out tonight to join in celebrating our upcoming wedding. I also must thank my good friends, who are now more like sisters, Kelly and Andrea, for putting together such a beautiful event. I love you both. I'm sure some of you have noticed something different about me as I walked around earlier or wondered why I raised up a glass of water during the toast. Not only are Kayne and I celebrating our engagement, we've already started our family. I'm pregnant." I smiled, moving my arms under my belly so everyone would really see the baby. Everyone clapped and cheered. All of the women rushed toward me to rub my stomach and give me their baby advice. Our happiness and cheers were suddenly interrupted by a commotion over by the glass double doors that led out onto the deck.

"That bitch is a man-stealing home wrecker! I hope you lose that bastard you're carrying!"

I recognized Marla's voice. She looked like a completely different person. Her face was broken out with ash, and her hair was dusty. Her tank top looked like it was originally white, but it now was gray from dirt and Lord knows what else. She had a crazed look in her eyes, a look of desperation and death. The restaurant manager began pulling her away from the door. Everyone watched in confusion as she continued to scream.

"Bitch, I hope you die!" I pushed past the group of women who had me circled and headed over to Marla. I was followed by my mother, Kelly and Kayne. Butter stayed behind to explain that Marla was an unstable addict. I heard the DJ start playing music in an attempt to distract everyone and get them back into a celebratory mood.

"Being arrested once didn't teach you a lesson?" Kayne asked, holding me back as Kelly tried to restrain me, too. My mother looked on, confused. Damen and Zelle looked ready to jump in and beat Marla down, even though she was a woman. "Call the cops," Kayne instructed my mother.

"I came to give you a gift," Marla slurred. I realized she was drunk as she pulled out a pocket knife and cut her arm right there in front of us. She lunged toward us. Kayne ripped a table cloth from off a nearby table and tackled her, wrapping her in the sheet like a baby. He sat on top of her. Marla was pinned down, but her legs were kicking around as she yelled and spat. Terrified, I backed up, pulling my mother and Kelly with me.

"Baby, are you okay?" I yelled to Kayne from behind Kelly and my mom.

"Yeah, I'm fine. Where the fuck are the cops?" he asked, out of breath.

"They said they are on their way," said my mom.

"Get off of me!" Marla yelled. The handful of people who were dining inside were now fixed on our drama. "You did this to me. I hate you!" Somehow Marla wiggled enough to where she could reach Kayne and bit him on the arm.

"Fuck!" Kayne jumped up, freeing Marla. She threw the blood soaked sheet at us. We dodged it and ran back outside, closing the glass doors behind us. She grabbed a chair and threw it through the glass. Before she could come out onto the deck, the police rushed in and the party was over. Kayne pulled them over to the side to tell them that she was HIV positive, and they called for backup. With plastic gloves on, they cuffed her, bandaged the wound and strapped her to a stretcher. The whole time she cried, beg-

ging Kayne to come back to her.

"Baby, please don't let them do this. Just come home. Leave that dirty bitch! If you don't, I'll kill you and her! No, I'll kill myself, I know you don't want me to do that, baby. I can't live without you!" she yelled out as the EMT workers loaded her into the ambulance. After they pulled off, I went back into the party only to thank everyone again for coming and to say my goodbyes. I was beyond embarrassed and ready to get home to pack my shit and make the move to Cali. I told Kayne on our way home that I didn't want to spend another minute in Cincinnati. All of the wedding plans were complete. I was ready to go.

Chapter 30

Saturday—June 2, 2007

I had already begun packing as many boxes as I could before Kelly and Trina arrived at my apartment to help. I was glad when Kelly told me the day before that she and Zelle had worked through the difficulty they had been having. Zelle knew now that Kelly was dedicated to him and only him.

"Damn, girl, you got a big load!" Trina laughed as she and Kelly walked through the door.

"I see you already started," Kelly said, looking around at five boxes that I already had filled and labeled.

"Yep, I'm ready to go!"

"Don't be so anxious to leave me, damn!" Kelly joked.

"You know I'm going to miss you both." I smiled and headed to the kitchen where I had everything from my cab-

inets sitting out, ready to be boxed.

"Can y'all pack the kitchen up for me while I finish packing the rest of my clothes and shoes?"

"Yeah. This won't even take long in here," Kelly said, grabbing a bottled water from the refrigerator.

"Good, because I need some help with my clothes, too, or I probably will never finish."

"Well, get prepared to donate some Gucci 'cause I know you don't need all that shit you got in there," Kelly joked.

"I got some cute stuff I'll put aside for both of y'all," I confirmed, really referring to the gifts I had purchased them.

"Okay, we got something for you, too. You're going to love it!" Kelly smiled, looking at Trina who smiled back. I was going to miss them both so much. Back in the day, the three of us were inseparable. Trina had moved while I was away, but she spent the last week in Cincinnati to visit and help with the wedding.

"Y'all two are so sweet. I can't wait to see it," I said.

"Oh, we know ..." Trina laughed.

As I was taking folded up sweaters down from the shelf in my oversized walk-in closet, I discovered my old photo albums that I had before I went away. I had put so many old pictures in there that I was sure most of them I had probably forgotten about.

I opened the blue photo album to find a baby picture of myself on the first page. It was an old Polaroid. I was sitting in my high chair at our old apartment back in the Bronx. I looked to be about one. I had a milk mustache surrounding my mouth and a cookie in my hand. I laughed as

I looked at the happy expression on my face. I looked like I thought that cookie was a million dollar prize. Funny how back then I was happy over the simplest things. I wished I could go back to that day even though right now I was the happiest I had ever been. I just wanted to feel that innocence again. It had been gone for so long. I wondered what it felt like to not need money, cars or clothes just to be truly happy. Feeling my baby girl kick in my stomach, I realized I would get that chance through her.

"Kelly! Trina! Come here!" I yelled, flipping through the album and coming across a picture of the three of us in elementary school, outside on the playground.

"What is it? We barely got started good," Kelly said, flopping down on my bed along with Trina.

"Look what I found." I handed her the photo album.

"Oh my goodness, look at us!" Kelly exclaimed.

"Look at Amina with that green and blue polka dot shirt on! She used to wear the life out that shirt." Trina and Kelly fell out laughing.

"Oh my God, didn't she!" Kelly agreed.

"Excuse me, but that was a special shirt, my grandmother brought me that from Hawaii," I said, trying to keep a straight face.

"We know, sweetie, but if it was so special you should have spared us and just put it up instead of putting it on every other day," Trina said as Kelly tried to control her laughter.

"Shut up! That shirt was hot. Y'all was just jealous." I chimed in laughing as I playfully smacked Trina in the head with a pillow.

"Okay, okay, and Kelly, you know you ain't off the hook. I got to let you know you was dead wrong for them purple jellies you had on with that white shirt and red shorts," Trina laughed.

"Yeah, I was wrong, but why did those yellow shorts even have to be that tight?" Kelly cracked on Trina.

"Because they was too little, and I didn't want to stop wearing them!" Trina said through uncontrollable laughter.

"Y'all so silly!" I shook my head.

"Look at us in our dresses for that club opening." Kelly flipped through more pages.

"Look at that expensive-ass Christian Dior dress Twin bought Mina." Trina took a closer look at the photo. Twin was my first sugar daddy. He bought me the dress to attend a club opening for his best friend in Columbus.

"Hell yeah, and she had the nerve to hook us up with them broke-ass niggas who had us in them cheap-ass mall dresses," Kelly said, smacking her lips.

"They wasn't broke. If they was Twin's friends, they was just cheap," I laughed, remembering how shocked Kelly and Trina were when they saw the dress I was wearing.

"Mina, didn't Twin take your virginity? Whatever happened to him? Y'all didn't really talk that long after that," Trina questioned.

"I thought he got locked up a few months later," Kelly commented, looking confused.

"No, that's just what I told you. He did take my virginity, but he broke my heart. I found out he had a girl and they had two kids together that he never told me about. It turned out I was just his little young fresh chick on the

side. I don't know if I ever told y'all, but he was the only other man I ever loved."

"You didn't have to tell us that, Mina. We're your friends. We knew that, but none of that matters now because you've got the man for you," Trina said confidently.

"Yeah, forget him." Kelly looked at the picture again. "He had a big head anyway." We all laughed.

"Look! Here's us painting your room at Zelle's old apartment," Kelly called out as I sat down next to her on the bed.

"Yeah, Zelle and I was just laughing about them shorts you had on trying to catch his eye that day." I laughed looking at the photo.

"And he was not giving my ass the time of day either." She laughed, remembering the day.

"You managed to get him anyway."

"Aww, here's us with Shayna at Damen's old mansion," Trina said, pointing to the photo of us sitting together in the home theater of my father's old house in Indian Hills.

"That was definitely a mansion. Here we are by the pool. Remember Shayna fixed us margaritas?" Kelly smirked.

"Yeah, that was the best time. I felt like a star on '*MTV Cribs*.'" Trina laughed.

"These are all you and Kayne in Puerto Rico," Kelly said, opening the other photo album I had grabbed out of my nightstand to be packed away.

"He really loved you even back then." Kelly smiled.

"Damn, is that the limo you rode in from the airport?" Trina asked, referring to the white stretch limo Kayne had

us ride in to the hotel.

"Yep, my baby gave me the best birthday ever that year." I smiled, remembering the perfect paradise I had shared with Kayne before my whole world came crashing down.

"I think I want to take a trip to the mountains after you told me how beautiful it was," Trina said, as Kelly closed the photo album.

"We should all go up there in the winter and rent a big chalet."

"That's a good idea. We could all spend New Year's there together," Kelly suggested.

"Yeah, that would be nice," Trina agreed.

"Let me show you what I put aside for you two." I went into my closet for two gift bags. "Here." I handed them each their own bag.

"Oooh, Louis!" Kelly sang, pulling a leather Louis Vuitton Onatah from her bag. "Thank you, I love it." She got up to hug me.

"You're welcome," I said as Trina pulled out her gift.

"A briefcase! Amina, this is so nice," Trina squealed excitedly, overlooking the signature Louis Vuitton embedded in the soft leather. "I never even thought about buying a briefcase. You make me feel like a real professional," she cheesed.

"I'm just getting you prepared, girl. You got to be a shrink with style!" We all laughed.

"I'll go get Mina's gift from the car." Kelly left the room. When she came back I was presented with a pink signature Coach baby bag equipped with a changing pad. Also inside was a cute teddy bear wearing a pink signature Coach bow tie.

"This is hot, and my baby got a Coach bear!"

"You know how we do—baby girl got to be fly, too!" Trina said.

"You was supposed to read the card first!" Kelly said.

"Ooops, I didn't see it." I opened the beautiful card that read: We Will Miss You. Inside, Kelly and Trina had written their own words:

> *Amina,*
>
> *First, I must say that I am both proud of you and happy for you. You have become such a good and strong woman over the years that we have grown together. I will miss you so much, but as a friend I know I could never lose you. So I'm wishing you the very best in your life. I know it will be as beautiful as you are. I love you like the sister you have become.*
>
> *Love,*
> *Kelly*

The other side read:

> *Amina,*
>
> *Over these eleven years that I have called you a friend, I am now realizing that you deserve to be called a sister. The time we were apart doesn't even compare to the time we have spent together, and I know that no matter how many miles away you are we will always be close. I love you and wish you the*

best on your marriage, child, career and brand new life.
- Trina

"This is really the sweetest card I've ever been given. And you know I love you both like sisters and will miss you both so much." Tears gathered in my eyes without permission. I hugged them both, causing their emotions to pour tears from their eyes, too.

"Looking at that picture of us back in fifth grade made me wonder how these years could have gone so fast," Kelly said.

"We're all grown up," Trina confirmed, smiling at us both.

"Thinking of us all being so far apart is making me wish we could just go back to that day on the playground just to stay together," I said through tears.

"We can be together whenever we want. It only takes a plane ticket and some time," Trina reminded me, putting her arm around my neck as I dried tears from my eyes.

"A plane ticket is no problem, but we all need to promise each other to always have time," Kelly said seriously.

"I promise," I told both of them.

"I promise." Trina smiled.

"And I promise," Kelly said.

"We'll always be sisters," I assured them.

Chapter 31

Saturday—July 7, 2007

Today I would be married to the only man I ever truly loved, the man who was going to stand before God and promise to take care of me for the rest of my life. I stood in front of my bedroom mirror with Kelly and Butter both standing beside me, making sure I was flawless. My off-white backless dress tied around my neck. It had been altered to fit my eight month pregnant belly perfectly. Luckily, I was all stomach and could pull off the dress without looking like a beached whale. My hair was swept into a side bun with a peach-colored flower stuck in the middle.

"You look beautiful, Amina," Kelly said, hugging me.

"Yes, you're gorgeous." Butter smiled.

"Thank you. You both look beautiful, too. Now let's just hope Marla doesn't crash the wedding!" I laughed alone as

I noticed the solemn looks on their faces. "It was a joke," I said, waiting for them to laugh along. My stomach tightened as I observed their expressions. "What?"

"I didn't want to tell you this, but—"

"But what?" I began to panic. Was this bitch going to ruin my wedding day? "Don't tell me that bitch is out there because if she is ... I swear, I'll kill her."

"We know, Amina." Butter was now looking over my shoulder and into the mirror with me. "Marla's dead."

"What?" I said, utterly surprised. "I had no idea." I sat down on the bed.

"After Shalauna got popped, Marla had nowhere to go. She tried to go back to Jason, but he was out of the closet. One night she went to his house, knocked on the door, shot him in the head and then turned the gun on herself."

"When did this happen?" I asked in disbelief.

"Three weeks ago," said Kelly.

"Does Kayne know?"

"Yes, he's the one who asked Butter and I not to tell you." Kelly clapped her hands. "Enough with the sadness. Come on, girl, let's get you down that aisle. I don't think Kayne can wait any longer."

Butter's cell phone rang. "The limo is outside." She closed her phone and slipped on her shoes. We rode in two all white Lincoln Navigator limousines to the beach where our family and friends had all joined to witness us take our vows. Watching the bridesmaids and groomsmen walk down the aisle first, I felt so amazed by the sheer perfection my wedding turned out to be. Everyone, including the guests, looked like they had stepped straight out of a mag-

azine.

Everyone stood to watch Damen escort me down the aisle to Kayne, who waited with a proud smile. Kayne and I wrote our own vows. I went first.

"Kayne, the first day I met you I knew that I would fall in love with you. Every day that we have spent together has felt like heaven, but nothing can compare to this day. I give myself to you completely. I know that you are whole, but I still want to complete you. I know that you are already a man, but I want to help you grow. And as your down chick, mother of your child and wife, I will always and forever be whatever you want and need. I love you now and forever." I smiled through tears, staring into his eyes, which never left mine as I spoke.

"Amina, you are everything a man could ever dream of. Your love and loyalty are so sweet it's almost unreal, but I know from experience that everything about you is real. Your beauty is unmatched and your heart is bigger than the world. We've been through storms that tried to tear us apart, but we're standing here together—unstoppable, unbreakable. Baby, I want to tell you you're irreplaceable. I love you, and I'll forever cherish you."

"I now pronounce you husband and wife," the preacher announced. I kissed Kayne with every ounce of passion in my body.

Everyone cheered as we walked back down the aisle. We went to the tent where the reception was to take place. While we sat at the head table, everyone came to greet us and the rest of the wedding party. Kelly sat next to Zelle sporting her brand new engagement ring, which Zelle had

given her a week ago. I was so happy for them. My mother and Gary were living together now in a brand new house and talking about marriage. They came to greet us first.

"Everything was perfect, baby." She kissed me and rubbed my cheek to remove her lipstick. "You look so beautiful." She turned to Kayne. "Son-in-law." She laughed at the sound of that. "Congratulations, I love you both."

Kayne's mom, Carla, came over next and handed Kayne an envelope. "Open it whenever you want, baby," she said, kissing him on the cheek.

After we cut the cake, the real fun began. Although I was the biggest thing on the dance floor, I could still work it. After our first dance, Kayne led me outside of the tent near the shore. I grabbed the envelope Carla had given him.

"Baby, open the gift from your mother," I said with excitement.

"You know what it is?" he asked as he tore into the envelope.

"Maybe." I smiled.

"Seventy thousand dollars?" In his hand, he held a check.

"It's a trust fund for the baby," I explained.

"I can't believe this. Where did my mama get all this money?"

"She's been saving it since she moved here from Chicago. She put money aside every chance she could just in case something were to happen."

"Damn, I can't believe she did this for me."

"She loves you, baby, and so do I." I grabbed his face

and kissed his lips.

"I love you, too. Open this," he said, handing me a small ring box.

"What could this be?" I asked, confused.

"Look and see." I opened the tiny box to find a key inside.

"Baby, what's this?"

"The key to your book store." He gave me a wide smile.

"Oh my God! Baby, thank you so much!"

"Now you have everything you ever wanted." He beamed.

"I can't imagine things being any more perfect, baby." I looked into his eyes. "Promise me it will stay this way. Promise me you'll never leave."

"I promise, baby. I can't think of anywhere else I would ever want to be."

ORDER FORM

Triple Crown Publications
PO Box 6888
Columbus, Oh 43205

Name: ______________________

Address: ______________________

City/State: ______________________

Zip: ______________________

	TITLES	PRICES
	Dime Piece	$15.00
	Gangsta	$15.00
	Let That Be The Reason	$15.00
	A Hustler's Wife	$15.00
	The Game	$15.00
	Black	$15.00
	Dollar Bill	$15.00
	A Project Chick	$15.00
	Road Dawgz	$15.00
	Blinded	$15.00
	Diva	$15.00
	Sheisty	$15.00
	Grimey	$15.00
	Me & My Boyfriend	$15.00
	Larceny	$15.00
	Rage Times Fury	$15.00
	A Hood Legend	$15.00
	Flipside of The Game	$15.00
	Menage's Way	$15.00

SHIPPING/HANDLING (Via U.S. Media Mail) **$3.95 1-2 Books, $5.95 3-4 Books add $1.95 for ea. additional book**

TOTAL **$**________

FORMS OF ACCEPTED PAYMENTS:

Postage Stamps, Institutional Checks & Money Orders, all mail in orders take 5-7 Business days to be delivered.

ORDER FORM

Triple Crown Publications
PO Box 6888
Columbus, Oh 43205

Name: ____________________

Address: ____________________

City/State: ____________________

Zip: ____________________

	TITLES	PRICES
	Still Sheisty	$15.00
	Chyna Black	$15.00
	Game Over	$15.00
	Cash Money	$15.00
	Crack Head	$15.00
	For The Strength of You	$15.00
	Down Chick	$15.00
	Dirty South	$15.00
	Cream	$15.00
	Hoodwinked	$15.00
	Bitch	$15.00
	Stacy	$15.00
	Life	$15.00
	Keisha	$15.00
	Mina's Joint	$15.00
	How To Succeed in The Publishing Game	$20.00
	Love & Loyalty	$15.00
	Whore	$15.00
	A Hustler's Son	$15.00

SHIPPING/HANDLING (Via U.S. Media Mail) **$3.95 1-2 Books, $5.95 3-4 Books add $1.95 for ea. additional book**

TOTAL $__________

FORMS OF ACCEPTED PAYMENTS:

Postage Stamps, Institutional Checks & Money Orders, all mail in orders take 5-7 Business days to be delivered.

ORDER FORM

Triple Crown Publications
PO Box 6888
Columbus, Oh 43205

Name: ______________________

Address: ______________________

City/State: ______________________

Zip: ______________________

	TITLES	PRICES
	Chances	$15.00
	Contagious	$15.00
	Hold U Down	$15.00
	Black and Ugly	$15.00
	In Cahootz	$15.00
	Dirty Red *Hardcover Only*	$20.00
	Dangerous	$15.00
	Street Love	$15.00
	Sunshine & Rain	$15.00
	Bitch Reloaded	$15.00
	Dirty Red *Paperback*	$15.00
	Mistress of the Game	$15.00
	Queen	$15.00
	The Set Up	$15.00
	Torn	$15.00
	Stained Cotton	$15.00
	Grindin *Hardcover Only*	$10.00

SHIPPING/HANDLING (Via U.S. Media Mail) **$3.95 1-2 Books, $5.95 3-4 Books add $1.95 for ea. additional book**

TOTAL $________

FORMS OF ACCEPTED PAYMENTS:

Postage Stamps, Institutional Checks & Money Orders, all mail in orders take 5-7 Business days to be delivered.